Charles King

A war-time wooing

Charles King

A war-time wooing

ISBN/EAN: 9783743367623

Manufactured in Europe, USA, Canada, Australia, Japa

Cover: Foto ©Andreas Hilbeck / pixelio.de

Manufactured and distributed by brebook publishing software (www.brebook.com)

Charles King

A war-time wooing

A WAR-TIME WOOING

"Colonel Putnam raises to the light of the first lantern a hairy, bushy object."—[See p. 50.]

A WAR-TIME WOOING

A Story

BY

CAPTAIN CHARLES KING, U. S. A.

ILLUSTRATED

NEW YORK

HARPER & BROTHERS, FRANKLIN SQUARE

ILLUSTRATIONS.

A WAR-TIME WOOING.

AFTER months of disaster there had come
authentic news of victory. All Union-loving
men drew a long breath of relief when it was
certain that Lee had given up the field and fallen
back across the Potomac. The newsboys, yelling
through the crowded streets in town, and the
evening trains arriving from the neighboring
city were besieged by eager buyers of the "ex-
tras," giving lists of the killed and wounded.
Just at sunset of this late September day a tall
young girl, in deep mourning, stood at a suburban
station clinging to the arm of a sad, stern-featured
old man. People eyed them with respect and
sympathy, not unmixed with rural curiosity, for
Doctor Warren was known and honored by one
and all. A few months agone his only son had

1

been brought home; shot to death at the head of
his regiment, and was laid in his soldier grave in
their shaded churchyard. It was a bitter trial,
but the old man bore up sturdily. He was an
eager patriot; he had no other son to send to the
front and was himself too old to serve; it had
pleased God to demand his first-born in sacrifice
upon his country's altar, and though it crushed
his heart it could not kill his loyalty and devotion. His whole soul seemed with the army in
Virginia; he had nothing but scorn for those
who lagged at home, nothing but enthusiastic
faith in every man who sought the battle-front, and
so it happened that he almost welcomed the indica-
tions that told him his daughter's heart was going
fast—given in return for that of a soldier lover.

For a moment it had dazed him. She was still
so young—so much a child in his fond eyes—still
his sweet-faced, sunny-haired baby Bess. He
could hardly realize she was eighteen even when
with blushing cheeks she came to show him the
photograph of a manly, gallant-looking young
soldier in the uniform of a lieutenant of infantry.
Strange as the story may seem to-day, there was
at the time nothing very surprising about its most
salient feature—she and her hero had never met.

With other girls she had joined a "Soldiers' Aid Society;" had wrought with devoted though misguided diligence in the manufacture of "Havelocks" that were bearers of much sentiment but no especial benefit to the recipients at the front; and like many of her companions she had slipped her name and address into one of these soon-discarded cap covers. As luck would have it, their package of "Havelocks," "housewives," needle-cases, mittens (with trigger finger duly provided for), ear-muffs, wristlets, knitted socks, and such things, worn by the "boys" their first winter in Virginia, but discarded for the regulation outfit thereafter, fell to the lot of the —th Massachusetts Infantry, and a courteous letter from the adjutant told of its distribution. Bessie Warren was secretary of the society, and the secretary was instructed to write to the adjutant and say how gratified they were to find their efforts so kindly appreciated. More than one of the girls wished that *she* were secretary just then, and all of them hoped the adjutant would answer. He did, and sent, moreover, a photographic group of several officers taken at regimental headquarters. Each figure was numbered, and on the back was an explana-

A*

tion setting forth the names of the officers, the item which each had received as his share, and, where it was known, the name of the fair manufacturer. The really useful items, it would seem, had been handed to the enlisted men, and the officers had reserved for themselves only such articles as experience had proved to be of no practical value. The six in the picture had all chosen "Havelocks," and opposite the name of Bessie Warren was that of Second Lieutenant Paul Revere Abbot. Reference to the "group" again developed the fact that Mr. Abbot was decidedly the handsomest soldier of the party—tall, slender, youthful, with clear-cut and resolute features and a decidedly firm, solid look about him that was distinguishable in a group of decidedly distinguished-looking men. There followed much laughing talk and speculation and theory among the girls, but the secretary was instructed to write another letter of thanks, and did so very charmingly, and mention was made of the circumstance that several of their number had brothers or cousins at the front. Then some of the society had happened, too, to have a photograph taken in the quaint uniform, with cap and apron, which they had worn at a recently given

"Soldiers' Fair," and one of their number—not Miss Warren—sent a copy of this to the camp of the —th Massachusetts. Central figure in this group was Bessie Warren, unquestionably the loveliest girl among them all, and one day there came to her a single photograph, a still handsomer picture of Mr. Paul Revere Abbot, and a letter in a hand somewhat stiff and cramped, in which the writer apologized for the appearance of the scrawl, explained that his hand had been injured while practising fencing with a comrade, but that having seen her picture in the group he could not but congratulate himself on having received a "Havelock" from hands so fair, could not resist the impulse to write and personally thank her, and then to inquire if she was a sister of Guthrie Warren, whom he had known and looked up to at Harvard as a "soph" looks up to a senior; and he enclosed his picture, which would perhaps recall him to Guthrie's mind.

Her mother had been dead many years, and Bessie showed this letter to her father, and with his full consent and with much sisterly pride wrote that Guthrie was indeed her brother; that he, too, had taken up arms for his country and was at the front with his regiment, though no-

where near their friends of the —th Massachusetts (who were watching the fords of the Potomac up near Edward's Ferry), and that she
had sent the photograph to him.

One letter seemed to lead to another, and those
from the Potomac speedily became very interesting, especially when the papers mentioned how
gallantly Lieutenant Paul Abbot had behaved at
Ball's Bluff and how hard he had tried to save
his colonel, who was taken prisoner. Guthrie returned the photograph to Bess, with a letter
which the doctor read attentively. He remembered Paul Abbot as being a leader in the younger set at Harvard, and was delighted to hear of
him "under the colors," where every Union-loving man should be—where, as he recalled him, he
knew Abbot must be, for he belonged to one of the
oldest and best families in all Massachusetts; he
was a gentleman born and bred, and would make
a name for himself in this war. Guthrie only
wished there were some of that stamp in his own
regiment, but he feared that there were few who
had the stuff of which the Abbots were made—
there were too many ward politicians. "But
I've cast my lot with it and shall see it through,"
wrote Guthrie. Poor fellow! poor father! poor

loving-hearted Bessie! The first volley from the crouching gray ranks in those dim woods back of Seven Pines sent the ward politicians in mad rush to the rear, and when Guthrie Warren sprang for the colors, and waved them high in air, and shouted for the men to rally and follow him, it was all in vain—all as vain as the effort to stop the firing made by the chivalric Virginia colonel, who leaped forward, with a few daring men at his back, to capture the resolute Yankee and his precious flag. They got them; but the life-blood was welling from the hero's breast as they raised him gently from the silken folds. The Virginians knew a brave man when they saw one, and they carried him tenderly into their lines and wrote his last messages, and that night they sent the honored body back to his brigade, and so the stricken father found and brought home all that was left of the gallant boy in whom his hopes were centred.

For a time Bessie's letters languished after this, though she had written nearly every week during the winter and early spring. Lieutenant Abbot, on the other hand, appeared to redouble his deep interest. His letters were full of sympathy—of a tenderness that seemed to be with difficulty repressed. She read these to her mourning father—they were so full of sorrow for the bitter loss that had befallen them, so rich with soldierly sentiment and with appreciation of Guthrie's heroic character and death, so welcome with reminiscence of him. Not that he and Abbot had met on the Peninsula—it was the unhappy lot of the Massachusetts —th to be held with McDowell's corps in front of Washington while their comrades were doing sharp, soldierly work down along the Chickahominy. But even where they were, said these letters, men talked by the hour of how Guthrie Warren had died at Seven Pines — how daring Phil Kearney himself had ridden up and held forth—

"The one hand still left,"

and asked him his name just before the final advance on the thicket. One letter contained a copy of some soldierly verses her Massachusett's correspondent had written—"Warren's Death at Seven Pines"—in which he placed him peer with Warren who fell at Bunker Hill. The verses thrilled through her heart and soul and brought a storm of tears—tears of mingled pride and love and hopeless sorrow from her aging father's eyes.

"The Virginians knew a brave man when they saw one."

No wonder she soon began to write more frequently. These letters from Virginia were the
greatest joy her father had, she told herself, and
though she wrote through a mist that blurred
the page, she soon grew conscious of a strange,
shy sense of comfort, of a thrilling little spring
of glad emotion, of tender, shrinking, sensitive
delight, and by the time the hot summer was
waning and August was at hand this unseen soldier, who had only shared her thoughts before,
took complete and utter control. Why tell the
old, old story in its every stage? It was with a
new, wild fear at heart she heard of Stonewall
Jackson's leap for the Rapidan, of the grapple
at Cedar Mountain where the Massachusetts men
fought sternly and met with cruel loss. Her
father raged with anxiety when the news came
of the withdrawal from the Peninsula, the tri-
umphant rush of Lee and Longstreet on Jackson's trail, of the ill-starred but heroic struggle
made by Pope along the banks of Bull Run. A
few days and nights of dread suspense and then
came tidings that Lee was across the Potomac
and McClellan marching to meet him. Two more
letters reached her from the marching —th
Massachusetts, and a telegram from Washington

telling her where to write, and saying, " All well so far as I am concerned," at which the doctor shook his head—it sounded so selfish at such a time; it grated on his patriotic ear, and it wasn't such as he thought an Abbot ought to telegraph. But then he was hurried; they probably only let him fall out of ranks a moment as they marched through Washington. And then the newspapers began to teem with details of the fierce battles of the last three days of August, and he forgave him and fathomed the secret in his daughter's breast as she stood breathing very quickly, her cheek flushing, her eyes filling, and listening while he read how Lieutenant Abbot had led the charge of the —th Massachusetts and seized the battle-flag of one of Starke's brigades at that bristling parapet—the old, unfinished railway grade to the north of Groveton. Neither father nor daughter uttered a word upon the subject. The old man simply opened his arms and took her to his heart, where, overcome with emotion, mingling pride and grief and anxiety and tender, budding love, she burst into tears and hid her burning face.

Then came the news of fierce fighting at South Mountain, where the —th Massachusetts was prominent; then of the Antietam, where twice it charged through that fearful stretch of cornfield and had but a handful left to guard the riddled colors when nightfall came, and then — silence and suspense. No letters, no news—nothing.

Her white, wan face and pleading eyes were too much for the father to see. Though no formal offer of marriage had been made, though the word "love" had hardly been written in those glowing letters, he reasoned rightly that love alone could prompt a man to write day after day in all the excitements and vicissitudes of stirring campaign. As for the rest—was he not an Abbot? Did not Guthrie know and honor him? Was he not a gallant officer as well as a thoroughbred gentleman? No time for wooing now! That would come with peace. He had even given his consent when she blushingly asked him if she might— "Well, *there!* read it yourself," she said, putting the closely written page into his hands. It was an eager plea for her picture—and the photograph was sent. He chose the one himself, a dainty "vignette" on card, for it reminded him of the mother who was gone. It was fitting, he told himself, that his daughter—her sainted mother's image, Guthrie's sister—should love a gallant soldier. He gloried in the accounts of Paul Abbot's bravery, and longed to meet him and take him by the hand. The time would come. He could wait and watch over the little girl who was drawing them together. He asked no questions. It would all be right.

And now they stood together at the station waiting for the evening cars and the latest news from the front. It lacked but a few minutes of train time when, with sad and sympathetic face, the station-agent approached, a fateful brown envelope in his hand. The doctor turned quickly at his daughter's gasping exclamation,

"*Papa!* Mr. Hardy has a telegram!"

Despite every effort his hand and lip trembled violently as he took it and tore it open. It was brief enough—an answer to his repeated despatches to the War Department.

"Lieutenant Paul R. Abbot, dangerously wounded, is at field hospital near Frederick, Maryland."

The doctor turned to her pale, pleading face, tears welling in his eyes.

"Be brave, my little girl," he murmured, brokenly. "He is wounded, but we can go to him at once."

Nearly sunset again, and the South Mountain is throwing its dark shadow clear across the Monocacy. The day has been warm, cloudless, beautiful, and, now that evening is approaching, the sentries begin to saunter out from the deeper shade that has lured them during the afternoon and to give a more soldierly tone to the picture. There are not many of them, to be sure, and this is evidently the encampment of no large command of troops, despite the number of big white tents pitched in the orchard, and the score of white-topped army-wagons, the half-dozen yellow ambulances, and the scraggy lot of mules in the pasture-lot across the dusty highway. The stream is close at hand, only a stone's-throw from the picturesque old farmhouse, and the animated talk among the groups of bathers has that peculiarly blasphemous flavor which seems inseparable from the average teamster. That the camp is under military tutelage is apparent from the fact that a tall young man in the loose, ill-fitting blue fatigue-dress of our volunteers, with war-worn belts and a business-like look to the long "Springfield" over his shoulder, comes striding down to the bank and shouts forthwith,

"You fellows are making too much noise there, and the doctor wants you to dry up."

"Tell him to send us some towels, then," growls one of the number, a black-browed, surly-looking fellow with ponderous, bent shoulders and a slouching mien. Some of his companions titter encouragingly, others are silent. The sergeant of the guard flushes angrily and turns on the speaker.

"You know very well what I mean, Rix. I'm using your own slang in speaking to you because you wouldn't comprehend decent language. It isn't the first time you've been warned not to make such a row here close to a lot of wounded and dying men. Now I mean business. Quit it or you'll get into trouble."

"What authority have *you* got, I'd like to know," is the sneering rejoinder. "You're nothing but a hospital guard, and have no business interfering with us. I ain't under no doctor's orders. You go back to your stiffs and leave live men alone."

The sergeant is about to speak, when the bathers, glancing up at the bank, see him suddenly face to his left and raise his hand to his shouldered rifle in salute. The next instant a tall young officer, leaning heavily on a cane and with his sword-arm in a sling, appears at the sergeant's side.

"Who is the man who questions your authority?" he asks, in a voice singularly calm and deliberate.

There is a moment's awkward silence. The sergeant has the reluctance of his class to getting a fellow-soldier into a scrape. The half-dressed bathers stand uncomfortably about the shore and look blankly from one to another. The man addressed as Rix is busily occupied in pulling on a pair of soldier brogans, and tying, with great deliberation, the leather strings.

Casting his clear eyes over the group, as he steps forward to the edge, the young officer speaks again:

"You're here, are you, Rix. That leaves little doubt as to the man even if I were not sure of the voice. I could hear your brutal swearing, sir, loud over the prayers the chaplain was saying for the dead. Have you no sense of decency at all?"

"How'n hell did I know there was any prayin' going on?" muttered Rix, bending his scowling brows down over his shoe and tugging savagely at the string.

"What was that remark, Rix?" asks the lieutenant, his grasp tightening on the stick.

No answer.

"Rix, drop that shoestring; stand attention, and look at me," says the officer, very quietly, but with setting teeth that no man fails to note. Rix slowly and sullenly obeys.

"What was the remark you made just now?" is again the question.

"I said I didn't know they were praying," growls Rix, finding he has to face the music.

"That sounds very little like your words, but —let it go. You knew very well that men were dying here right within earshot when you were making the air blue with blasphemy, and when better men were reverently silent. It is the third time you have been reprimanded in a week. I shall see to it that you are sent back to your company forthwith."

"Not while Lieutenant Hollins is quartermaster you won't," is the insubordinate reply, and even the teamsters look scared as they glance from the scowling, hanging face of Rix to the clear-cut features of the officer, and mark the change that sweeps over the latter. His eyes seem to flash fire, and his pallid face—thin with suffering and loss of blood—flushes despite his physical weakness. His handsome mouth sets like a steel-trap.

"Sergeant, get two of your men and put that fellow under guard," he orders. "Stay where you are, Rix, until they come for you." His voice is low and stern; he does not condescend to raise it for such occasion, though there is a something about it that tells the soldier-ear it can ring with command where ring is needed.

"I'd like to know what I've done," mutters Rix, angrily kicking at the pebbles at his feet.

No answer. The lieutenant has walked back a pace and has seated himself on a little bench. Another officer—a gray-haired and distinguished-looking man, with silver eagles on his shoulders—is rapidly nearing him and reaches the bank just in time to catch the next words. He could have heard them farther back, for Rix is in a fury now, and shouts aloud:

"If you knew your own interests—knew half that I know about your affairs, Lieutenant Abbot—you'd think twice before you ordered me under arrest."

The lieutenant half starts from the bench, but his self-control is strong.

2

"You are simply adding to your insubordination, sir," he says, coldly. "Take your prisoner, sergeant. You men are all witnesses to this language."

And muttering much to himself, Teamster Rix is marched slowly away, leaving an audience somewhat mystified. The colonel stands looking after him with a puzzled and astonished face; the men begin slowly to edge away, and then Mr. Abbot wearily rises and—again he flushes red when he finds his superior officer facing him at not three paces distance.

"What on earth does that mean, Abbot?" asks the colonel. "Who is that man?"

"One of the regimental teamsters, sir. He came here with the wounded, and there appears to have been no opportunity of sending him back now that the regiment is over in the Shenandoah. At all events, he has been allowed to loaf around here for some time, and you probably heard him swearing."

"I did; that's what brought me out of the house. But what does he mean by threatening you?"

"I have no idea, sir; or, rather, I have an idea, but the matter is of no consequence whatever, and only characteristic of the man. He is a scoundrel, I suspect, and I wonder that Hollins has kept him so long."

"Do you know that Hollins hasn't turned up yet?"

"So I heard this morning, colonel, and yet you saw him the night of the battle, did you not?"

"Not the night after, but the night before. We left him with the wagons when we marched to the ford. I was knocked off my horse about one in the afternoon, just north of the cornfield, and they got me back to the wagons with this left shoulder all out of shape—collar-bone broken; and he wasn't there then, and hadn't been seen since daybreak. Somebody said he was so cut up when you were hit at the Gap. I didn't know you were such friends."

"Well, we've known each other a long time—were together at Harvard and moved in the same set; but there was never any intimacy, colonel."

"I see, I see," says the older officer, reflectively. "He was a stranger to me when I joined the regiment and found him quartermaster. He was Colonel Raymond's choice, and you know that in

B

succeeding to his place I preferred to make no changes. But I say to you now that I wish I had. Hollins has failed to come up to the standard as a campaign quartermaster, and the men have suffered through his neglect more than once. Then he stayed behind when we marched through Washington—a thing he never satisfactorily explained to me—and I had serious thoughts of relieving him at Frederick and appointing you to act in his stead. Now the fortune of war has settled both questions. Hollins is missing, and you are a captain or will be within the month. Have you heard from Wendell?"

"His arm is gone, sir; amputated above the elbow; and he has decided to resign. Foster commands the company, but I shall go forward just as soon as the doctor will let me."

"We'll go together. He says I can stand the ride in ten days or two weeks, but neither of your wounds has healed yet. How's the leg? That must have been a narrow squeak."

"No bones were touched, sir. It was only that I lost so much blood from the two. It was the major who reported me to you as dangerously wounded, was it not?"

"Yes; but when he left you there seemed to

be very little chance. You were senseless and exhausted, and with two rifle bullets through you what was to be expected? He couldn't tell that they happened to graze no artery, and the surgeon was too busy elsewhere."

"It gave them a scare at home," said Abbot, smiling; "and my father and sister were on the point of starting for Washington when I managed to send word to them that the wounds were slight. I want to get back to the regiment before they find out that they were comparatively serious, because the family will be importuning the Secretary of War to send me home on leave."

"And any man of your age, with such a home, and a sweetheart, ought to be eager to go. Why not go, Abbot? There will be no more fighting for months now; McClellan has let them slip. You could have a fortnight in Boston as well as not, and wear your captain's bars for the first time. I fancy I know how proud Miss Winthrop would be to sew them on for you."

The colonel is leaning against the trunk of a spreading oak-tree as he speaks. The sun is down, and twilight closing around them. Mr. Abbot, who had somewhat wearily reseated himself on the rude wooden bench a moment before, has turned gradually away from the speaker during these words, and is gazing down the beautiful valley. Lights are beginning to twinkle here and there in the distance, and the gleam of one or two tiny fires tells of other camps not far away. A dim mist of dust is rising from the highroad close to the stream, and a quaint old Maryland cabriolet, drawn by a venerable gray horse, is slowly coming around the bend. The soldiers grouped about the gateway, back at the farmhouse, turn and look curiously towards the hollow-sounding hoof-beats, but neither the colonel nor his junior officer seems to notice them. Abbot's thoughts are evidently far away, and he makes no reply. The surgeon who sanctions his return to field duty yet a while would, to all appearances, be guilty of a professional blunder. The lieutenant's face is pale and thin; his hand looks very fragile and fearfully white in contrast with the bronze of his cheek. He leans his head upon his hand as he gazes away into the distance, and the colonel stands attentively regarding him. He recalls the young fellow's gallant and spirited conduct at Manassas and South Mountain; his devotion to his soldier duty since the day he first " reported." If ever an officer deserved a month

at home, in which to recuperate from the shock
of painful wounds, surely that officer was Abbot.
The colonel well knows with what pride and
blessing his revered old father would welcome
his coming—the joy it would bring to the household at his home. It is an open secret, too, that
he is engaged to Genevieve Winthrop, and surely
a man must want to see the lady of his love. He
well remembers how she came with other ladies
to attend the presentation of colors to the regiment, and how handsome and distinguished a
woman she looked. The Common was thronged
with Boston's "oldest and best" that day, and
Colonel Raymond's speech of acceptance made
eloquent reference to the fact that of all the
grand old names that had been prominent in the
colonial history of the commonwealth not one
was absent from the muster-roll of the regiment
it was his high honor to command. The Abbots and Winthrops had a history coeval with
that of the colony, and were long and intimately
acquainted. When, therefore, it was rumored
that Genevieve Winthrop was to marry Paul
Abbot "as soon as the war was over," people
simply took it as a matter of course—they had
been engaged ever since they were trundled side

by side in the primitive baby-carriages of the earliest forties. This reflection leads the colonel to the realization of the fact that they must be very much of an age. Indeed, had he not heard it whispered that Miss Winthrop was the senior by nearly a year? Abbot looked young, almost boyish, when he was first commissioned in May of '61, but he had aged rapidly, and was greatly changed. He had not shaved since June, and a beard of four months' growth had covered his face. There are lines in his forehead, too, that one could not detect a year before. Why should not the young fellow have a few weeks' leave, thinks the colonel. The regiment is now in camp over beyond Harper's Ferry, greatly diminished in numbers and waiting for its promised recruits. It is evident that McClellan has no intention of attacking Lee again; he is content with having persuaded him to retire from Maryland. Nothing will be so apt to build up the strength and spirits of the new captain as to send him home to be lionized and petted as he deserves to be. Doubtless all the languor and sadness the colonel has noted in him of late is but the outward and visible sign of a longing for home which he is ashamed to confess.

"Abbot," he says again, suddenly and abruptly, "I'm going back to Frederick this evening as soon as the medical director is ready, and I'm going to get him to give you a certificate on which to base application for a month's leave. Don't say no. I understand your scruples, but go you shall. You richly deserve it and will be all the better for it. Now your people won't have to be importuning the War Department; the leave shall come from this end of the line."

The lieutenant seems about to turn again as though to thank his commander when there comes an interruption—the voice of the sergeant of the guard close at hand. He holds forth a card; salutes, and says:

"A gentleman inquiring for Colonel Putnam."

And the gentleman is but a step or two behind—an aging man with silvery hair and beard, with lines of sorrow in his refined and scholarly face, and fatigue and anxiety easily discernible in his bent figure—a gentleman evidently, and the colonel turns courteously to greet him.

"Doctor Warren!" he says, interrogatively, as he holds forth his hand.

"Yes, colonel, they told me you were about going back to Frederick, and I desired to see you

at once. I am greatly interested in a young officer of your regiment who is here, wounded; he is
a college friend of my only son's, sir—Guthrie
Warren, killed at Seven Pines." The colonel
lifts his forage cap with one hand while the other
more tightly clasps that of the older man." I
hear that the reports were exaggerated and that
he is able to be about. It is Lieutenant Abbot."

"Judge for yourself, doctor," is the smiling
reply. "Here he sits."

With an eager light in his eyes the old gentleman steps forward towards Abbot, who is
slowly rising from the bench. He, too, courteously raises his forage cap. In a moment both
the doctor's hands have clasped the thin, white
hand that leans so heavily on the stick.

"My dear young friend!" he says. "My gallant boy! Thank God it is not what we feared!"
and his eyes are filling, his lip is trembling painfully.

"You are very kind, sir," says Abbot, vaguely,
"I am doing quite well." Then he pauses.
There is such yearning and—something he cannot fathom in the old man's face. He feels that
he is expected to say still more—that this is not
the welcome looked for. "I beg a thousand par-

dons, sir, perhaps I did not catch the name aright. Did you say Doctor Warren?"

"Certainly, B— Guthrie Warren's father—you remember?" and the look in the sad old eyes is one of strange perplexity. "I cannot thank you half enough for all you have written of my boy."

And still there is no sign of recognition in Abbot's face. He is courteous, sympathetic, but it is all too evident that there is something grievously lacking.

"I fear there is some mistake," he gently says; "I have no recollection of knowing or writing of any one of that name."

"Mistake! Good God! How can there be?" is the gasping response. The tired old eyes are ablaze with grief, bewilderment, and dread commingled. "Surely this is Lieutenant Paul Revere Abbot—of the —th Massachusetts."

"It certainly is, doctor, but—"

"It surely is your photograph we have: surely you wrote to—to us all this last year—letter after letter about my boy—my Guthrie."

There is an instant of silence that is almost agonizing. The colonel stands like one in a state of shock. The old doctor, trembling from head

B*

to foot, looks with almost piteous entreaty; with anguish and incredulity, and half - awakened wrath, into the pale and distressed features of the young soldier.

"I bitterly grieve to have to tell you, sir," is the sorrowful answer, "but I know no such name. I have written no such letters."

Another instant, and the old man has dropped heavily upon the bench, and buried his face in his arms. But for the colonel he might have fallen prone to earth.

II.

An hour after sundown and the rattling old cabriolet has two occupants as it drives back to town. Colonel Putnam comes forth with the old gentleman whom he had so tenderly conducted to the farmhouse but a few moments after the strange scene out on the bank, and is now his escort to Frederick. The sergeant of the guard has been besieged with questions, for several of the men saw the doctor drop upon the bench and were aware of the melodramatic nature of the meeting. Lieutenant Abbot with a face paler than before, with a strange look of perplexity and smouldering wrath about his handsome eyes, has gone over to his own tent, where the surgeon presently visits him. The colonel and his civilian visitor are closeted together over half an hour, and the latter looks more dead than alive, say the men, as he feebly totters down the steps clinging to the colonel's arm.

"What did you say was the name of the officer

who was killed—his son?" asks one of the guards as he stands at the entrance to the tent.

"Warren—Guthrie Warren," answers the sergeant, briefly. "I don't know whether the old man's crazy or not. He said the lieutenant had been writing to him for months about his son, and the lieutenant denied having written a line."

"He lied then, by —— !" comes a savage growl from within the tent. "Where is the old man? Give me a look at him!" and the scowling face of Rix makes its sudden appearance at the tent-flop, peering forth into the fire-light.

"Be quiet, Rix, and go back where you belong. You've made more than enough trouble to-day," is the sergeant's low-toned order.

"I tell you I only want to see the old man," answers the teamster, struggling, "Don't you threaten me with that bayonet, Drake," he growls savagely at the sentry, who has thrown himself in front of the opening. "It'll be the worse for you fellows that you ever confined me, no matter by whose order; but as for that stuck-up prig, by —— ! you'll see soon enough what'll come of *his* ordering me into the guard-tent."

His voice is so hoarse and loud with anger that the colonel's attention is attracted. He has just seated Doctor Warren in the vehicle, and is about to take his place by his side when Rix's tirade bursts upon his ear. The words are only partially distinguishable, but the colonel steps promptly back.

"What is the matter with your prisoner, sergeant? Is he drunk or crazy, that he persists in this uproar?"

"I don't think it either, sir," answers the sergeant; while Rix, at sight of his commanding officer, pops his head back within the tent, and shuts the narrow slit. "He's simply ugly and bent on making trouble."

"Well, stop it! If he utters another insubordinate word, have him bucked and gagged at once. He is disgracing the regiment, and I won't tolerate it. Do you understand?"

"I do, sir."

The colonel turns abruptly away, while the prisoner, knowing his man, keeps discreetly out of sight, and correspondingly silent. At the gate the older officer stops once more and calls to a soldier who is standing near.

"Give my compliments to Lieutenant Abbot, and say that I will be out here again to-morrow afternoon. Now, doctor, I am with you."

The old gentleman is leaning wearily back in his corner of the cab; a strange, stunned, lethargic feeling seems to have come over him. His eyes are fixed on vacancy, if anything, and the colonel's attempt at cheeriness meets no response. As the vehicle slowly rattles away he makes an effort, rouses himself as it were from a stupor-like condition, and abruptly speaks:

"You tell me that—that you have seen Lieutenant Abbot's mail all summer and spring and never saw a — our postmark—Hastings?"

"I have seen his mail very often, and thought his correspondents were all home people. I am sure I would have noticed any letters coming frequently in one handwriting, and his father's is the only masculine superscription that was at all regular.

"My letters—our home letters—were not often addressed by me," hesitates the doctor. "The postmark might have given you an idea. I had not time—" but he breaks off, weakly. It is so hard for him to prevaricate: and it is bitter as death to tell the truth, now. And worse—worse! What is he to tell—*how* is he to tell her?

The colonel speaks slowly and sadly, but with earnest conviction:

"No words can tell you how I mourn the heartlessness of this trick, doctor; but you may rest assured it is no doing of Abbot's. What earthly inducement could he have? Think of it! a man of his family and connections—and character, too. Some scoundrel has simply borrowed his name, possibly in the hope of bleeding you for money. Did none of the letters ever suggest embarrassments? It is most unfortunate that you did not bring them with you. I know the writing of every officer and many of the men in the regiment, and it would give me a clew with which to work. Promise me you will send them when you reach home."

The Doctor bows his head in deep dejection. "What good will it do? I thought to find a comrade of my boy's. Indeed! it must be one who knew him well!—and how can I desire to bring to punishment one who appreciated my son as this unknown writer evidently did. His only crime seems to have been a hesitancy about giving his own name."

"And a scoundrelly larceny of that of a better man in every way. No, doctor. The honor of my regiment demands that he be run down and brought to justice; and you must not withhold

3

the only proof with which we can reach him. Promise me!"

"I—I will think. I am all unstrung now, my dear sir! Pray do not press me! If it was not Mr. Abbot, who could it have been? Who else could have known him?"

"Why, Doctor Warren, there are probably fifty Harvard men in this one regiment—or were at least," says the colonel, sadly, "up to a month ago. Cedar Mountain, Bull Run, South Mountain, and Antietam have left but a moiety. Most of our officers are graduates of the old college, and many a man was there. I dare say I could have found a dozen who well knew your son. In the few words I had with Abbot, he told me he remembered that there had been some talk among the officers last July after your son was killed. Some one saw the name in the papers, and said that it must have been Warren of the class of '58, and our Captain Webster, who was killed at Manassas, was in that class and knew him well. Abbot said he remembered him, by sight, as a sophomore would know a senior, but had never spoken to him. Anybody hearing all the talk going on at the time we got the news of Seven Pines could have woven quite a college history out of it—and somebody has."

"Ah, colonel! There is still the fact of the photograph, and the letters that were written about Guthrie all last winter—long before Seven Pines."

The colonel looks utterly dejected, too; he shakes his head, mournfully. "That troubles Abbot as much as it does me. Fields, gallant fellow, was our adjutant then, and he and Abbot were close friends. He could hardly have had a hand in anything beyond the photograph and letter which, you tell me, were sent to the Soldier's Aid Society in town. I remember the young fellows were having quite a lot of fun about their Havelocks when we lay at Edwards's Ferry—but Fields was shot dead, almost the first man, at Cedar Mountain, and of the thirty-five officers we had when we crossed the Potomac the first time, only eleven are with the —th to-day. Abbot, who was a junior second lieutenant then, is a captain now, by rights, and daily expecting his promotion. I showed you several letters in his hand, and they, you admit, are utterly unlike the ones you received. Indeed, doctor, it is impossible to connect Abbot with it in any way."

The doctor's face is covered by his hands. In

ten minutes or less he must be at *her* side. What can he tell his little girl? What shall he say? What possible, probable story can man invent to cover a case so cruel as this? He hardly hears the colonel's words. He is thinking—thinking with a bursting heart and whirling brain. For a time all sense of the loss of his only son seems deadened in face of this undreamed-of, this almost incredible shadow that has come to blight the sweet and innocent life that is so infinitely dear to him. What can he say to Bessie when he meets those beautiful, pleading, trusting, anxious eyes? She has borne up so bravely, silently, patiently. Their journey has been trying and full of fatigue, but once at Frederick he has left her in the hands of a sympathetic woman, the wife of the proprietor of the only tavern in which a room could be had, and, promising to return as soon as he could see the lieutenant, he has gone away on his quest with hopeful heart. A soldier claiming to be of the —th Massachusetts told them that very morning at the Baltimore station that Mr. Abbot was well enough to be up and about. It is barely nine o'clock now. In less than an hour there will be a train going back. All he can think of is that they must go—go as quick as possible. They have nothing now to keep them here, and he has one secret to guard from all—his little girls'. No one must know, none suspect that. In the bitterness of desolation, still stunned and bewildered by the cruelty of the blow that has come upon them, his mind is clear on that point. If possible no one, except those people at the tavern, must know she was with him. None must suspect—above all—none must suspect the bitter truth. It would crush her like a bruised and trodden flower.

"If—if it had been a correspondence where there was a woman in the case," begins the colonel again—and the doctor starts as though stung, and his wrinkled hands wring each other under the heavy travelling-shawl he wears—"I could understand the thing better. Quite a number of romantic correspondences have grown up between our soldiers and young girls at home through the medium of these mittens and things; they seem to have lost their old significance. But you give me to understand that—that there was none?"

"The letters were solely about my son, all that ever came to me," said the doctor, nervously.

"That seems to complicate the matter. If it were a mere flirtation by letter, such as is occasionally going on, *then* somebody might have borrowed his name and stolen his photograph; but I don't see how he could have secured the replies—the girl's letters—in such a case. No. As you say, doctor, that wasn't apt to be the solution, though I'm at a loss to account for the letters that came from you. They were addressed to Lieutenant Abbot, camp of the —th Massachusetts, you tell me, and Abbot declares he has never heard from any one of your name, or had a letter from Hastings. He would be the last man, too, to get into a correspondence with a woman—for he is engaged."

The doctor starts again as though stung a second time. Was there not in one of those letters a paragraph over which his sweet daughter had blushed painfully as she strove to read it aloud? Did it not speak of an entanglement that once existed; an affair in which his heart had never been enlisted, but where family considerations and parental wishes had conspired to bring about a temporary " understanding " ? The cabriolet is bouncing about on the cobblestones of the old-fashioned street, and the doctor is thankful for the physical jar. Another moment and they draw up at the door of the old Maryland hostelry, and the colonel steps out and assists his companion to alight.

"Let me take you to your room now, doctor; then I'll have our staff surgeon come over and see you. It has been a shock which would break a younger man—"

But the old gentleman has nerved himself for the struggle. First and foremost—no one must follow him to his room—none suspect the trial there awaiting him. He turns sadly, but with decision.

"Colonel, I cannot thank you now as you deserve; once home, I will write, but now what I need is absolute rest a little while. I am stunned, bewildered. I must think this out, and my best plan is to get to sleep first. Forgive me, sir, for my apparent discourtesy, and do not take it amiss if I say that for a few moments—for the present—I should like to be alone. We—we will meet again, sir, if it rest with me, and I will write. Good-night, colonel. Good-night, sir."

And he turns hurriedly away. For a moment the soldier stands uncertain what to do. Then he enters the hallway determined to bespeak the best offices of the host in behalf of his stricken friend. There is a broad stairway some distance back in the hall, and up this he sees the doctor slowly laboring. He longs to go to his assistance, but stands irresolute, fearing to offend. The old gentleman nears the top, and is almost on the landing above, when a door is suddenly opened, a light, quick step is heard, and in an instant a tall, graceful girl, clad in deep black— a girl whom the colonel sees is young, beautiful, and very pale—springs forward into view, places her hands on the old man's shoulders, and looks eagerly, imploringly, into his face. What she asks, what she says, the colonel cannot hear; but another moment solves all doubt as to his proper course. He sees her clasped to the doctor's breast; he sees them clinging to each other one instant, and then the father, with sudden rally, bears her pale and probably fainting from his sight. A door shuts with muffled slam, and they are gone; and with the intuition of a gentleman Colonel Putnam realizes why his proffer of services would now be out of place.

"And so there is a woman in the case, after all," he thinks to himself as he steps forth into the cool evening air. "And it is for her sake the good old man shrinks from dragging the matter into the light of day—his daughter, probably; and some scoundrel has been at work, and in my regiment."

The colonel grinds his teeth and clinches his fists at this reflection. He is a husband and father himself, and now he understands some features in the old doctor's trouble which had puzzled him before. He strolls across the street to the sidewalk under the quaint old red-brick, dormer-windowed houses where lights are still gleaming, and where groups of people are chatting and laughing in the pleasant air. Many of them are in the rough uniform of the army —teamsters, drivers, and slightly wounded soldiers out on pass from the neighboring field hospitals. The old cabriolet is being trundled off to some neighboring stable after a brief confabulation between the driver thereof and the landlord of the tavern, and the colonel is about hailing and tendering the Jehu another job for the morrow, when he sees that somebody else is before him; and, bending down from his seat, the driver is talking with a man who has come out from the shadow of a side porch. There is but little light in the street, and the colonel has

turned on reaching the curb, and is seeking among
the windows across the way for one which may
possibly prove to be the young lady's. IIe is
interested in the case more than ever now, but
the windows give no sign. Some are lighted,
and occasional shadows flit across them, but none
that are familiar. Suddenly he hears a sound
that brings him back to himself—the tramp of
marching feet, and the sudden clash of arms as
they halt; a patrol from the provost-marshal's
guard comes quickly around a corner from the
soft dust of a side street, and the non-commis-
sioned officers are sharply halting all neighboring men in uniform, and examining their passes.
Several parties in army overcoats shuffle uneasily
up the street, only to fall into the clutches of· a
companion patrol that pops up as suddenly around
the next corner beyond. "Rounding up the
stragglers," thinks the colonel, with a quiet smile
of approval, and, like the soldier he is, he finds
time to look on a moment and watch the manner in which the work is done. The patrol seems
to have possessed itself of both sides of the
street at the same instant, and "spotted" every
man in blue. These are bidden to stand until
their papers are examined by the brace of young

officers who appear upon the scene, belted and sashed, and bearing small lanterns. Nor are uniforms alone subject to scrutiny. Ever since Second Bull-Run there has been much straggling in the army, and not a little desertion; and though a fortnight has passed since Antietam was fought, the provost-marshal's men have not yet finished scouring the country, and a sharp lookout is kept for deserters. Those civilians who can readily establish their identity as old residents of the town have no trouble. Occasionally a man is encountered whom nobody seems to know, and, despite their protestations, two of those characters have been gathered in by the patrol, and are now on their way to the office. The colonel hears their mingled complaint and blasphemy as they are marched past him by a file of the guard, and then turns to the nearest of the officers—

"Lieutenant, did you note the man who ran back from where that cab is standing?"

The officer of the patrol looks quickly up from the "pass" he is examining by the light of his lantern, and at sight of Colonel Putnam his hand goes up to the visor of his cap.

"No, colonel; was there one? Which way did he go?"

C

"Straight back to the shadow of the porch; just a minute ago. What attracted my attention to him was the fact that he was deep in talk with the driver when your men rounded the corner, and did not seem to see or hear them. Then I turned to look at that corporal yonder, as he crossed to halt a man on the east side, and at sound of his voice this fellow at the cab started suddenly and ran, crouching in the shadow, back to the side of the tavern there. It looks suspicious."

"Come with me, two of you," says the lieutenant, quickly, and, followed by a brace of his guard, he crosses the street, and his lantern is seen dancing around the dark gallery. The colonel, meantime, accosts the driver:

"What took that man away so suddenly? Who is he?"

"I don't know, sir. I never seen him afore. He stopped me right here to ask who the gentleman was I was drivin'. I told him your name, 'cause I heard it, and he started then kinder queer, but came back and said 'twas the citizen he meant; and the boss here had just told me that was Doctor Warren, and that his daughter was up-stairs. Then the feller jumped like he was scared; the guard had just come round the corner, and when he saw them he just put for the barn."

"Is there a barn back there?" asks the colonel. The driver nods assent. A moment's silence, and then the colonel continues: "I want to see you in the morning. Wait for me here at the hotel about nine o'clock. Meantime say nothing about this, and you'll lose nothing by holding your tongue. What was his face like—this man I mean?"

"Couldn't see it, sir. It was dark, and he had a beard all over it, and wore a black-felt hat—soft; and he had a cloak something like yours, that was wrapped all over his shoulders."

"Remember, I want to see you here in the morning; and hold your tongue till then."

With that the colonel hastens off on the trail of the searching-party. He sees the lantern glimmering among some dark buildings beyond the side-gallery, and thither he follows. To all appearances the spot is almost a *cul de sac* of wooden barns, board-fences, and locked doors, except for a gateway leading to the yard behind the tavern. The search has revealed no trace of the skulker, and the lieutenant holds his lamp aloft as he examines the gate and peers over the picket fence that stands barely breast-high and bars them out.

"May have gone in here," he mutters. "Come on!"

But the search here only reveals half a dozen avenues of escape. The man could have gone back through several doors into the building itself, or eastward, through some dilapidated yards, into a street that was uninfested by patrols, and dark as the bottom of a well. "It is useless to waste further time," says the lieutenant, who presently rejoins the colonel behind the tavern, and finds him staring up at the rear windows. To him the young officer, briefly and in low tone, reports the result of his search.

"I presume there is nothing else I can do just here, is there, colonel?" he asks. The colonel shakes his head.

"Nothing that I can think of, unless you look through the halls and office."

"We are going there. Shall I light you back to the street?"

"Er—ah—no! I think I'll wait here—just a moment," says the colonel, and, marvelling not a little, the subaltern leaves him.

No sooner is he gone, followed by his men,

than Colonel Putnam steps back to the side of
an old chain-pump that he has found in the course
of his researches, and here he leans for support.
Though his shoulder has set in shape, and is doing fairly well, he has had two rather long drives
this day, and one fatiguing experience; he is beginning to feel wearied, but is not yet ready to
go to his bed. That was Doctor Warren's shadow, bent and feeble, that he saw upon the yellow
light of the window-shade a moment ago, and he
is worried at the evidence of increasing weakness
and sorrow. Even while he rests there, irresolute as to what he ought to do—whether to go
and insist on his right, as a man and a father, to
be of some comfort to another in his sore trial,
or to respect that father's evident wish to conceal his daughter's interest in the trouble that
had come upon them—he is startled to see another shadow, hers; and this shadow is in hat
and veil. Whither can they be going at this hour
of the night? 'Tis nearly ten o'clock. Yes, surely; there is the doctor's bent shadow once more,
and he has thrown on an outer coat of some kind.
Then they are going back by the night train.
They shrink from having it known that she was
here at all; that she was in any way interested.

And the doctor wants to make his escape without the pang of seeing or being seen again by those who witnessed his utter shock and distress this day. So be it! thinks the colonel. God knows I would not intrude on the sanctity of his sorrow or her secret. Later, when they are home again, the matter can be looked into so far as getting specimens of this skulking felon's handwriting is concerned, and no one need know, when he is unearthed, that it was a young girl he was luring under the name of another man. So be it! They may easily elude all question now. Night and the sacred mantle of their evident suffering will shield them from observation or question.

The colonel draws deeper into the shade of the barn. It seems a sacrilege now to be thus spying upon their movements, and he is ashamed of the impulse that kept him there. He decides to leave the yard and betake himself to his lodgings, when he is suddenly aware of a dark object rising from under the back porch. Stealthily and slowly the figure comes crouching out into the open yard, coming towards where the colonel stands in the shadow of the black out-buildings; and then, when close by the pump where he stood but a moment before, it rises to its full height, and draws a long breath of relief. It is a man in a soft black-felt hat, with a heavy, dark beard, and wearing one of the biggest of the great circular capes that make a part of the officer's overcoat, and are most frequently worn without the coat itself, unless the weather be severe.

The colonel is unarmed; his pistols are over at the room he temporarily occupies in town; he is suffering from recent injury, and one arm is practically good for nothing, but he loses no time in lamenting these points. The slight form of the girl approaches the window at this very instant as though to pick up some object on the sill, then disappears, and the light vanishes from the room. From the figure at the pump he hears a stifled exclamation of surprise, but no articulate word; and before the figure has time to recover he stands close beside it and his voice breaks the stillness of the night.

"Your name, sir, and your regiment? I am Colonel Putnam."

He has laid his hand on the broad shoulder under the cloak and plainly feels the start and thrill with which his words are greeted. He even fancies he can hear the stifled word "God!"

4

The man seems stricken dumb, and more sharply the colonel begins his stern query a second time, but gets no farther than "Your name," when, with a violent wrench, the stranger is free; he makes a spring, trips over some loose rubbish, and goes crashing to earth.

"The guard!" yells the colonel, as he throws himself upon him, but the man is up in an instant, hurls off his antagonist, and, this time, leaps off into the darkness in comparative safety. But he has left a clew behind. As the soldiers of the provost guard come running around into the yard and the windows are thrown up and eager heads peer forth in excited inquiry, Colonel Putnam raises to the light of the first lantern a hairy, bushy object that he holds in his hand; it is a false beard, and a big one.

"By Jove!" says the lieutenant. "It must be some rebel spy."

III.

DAYBREAK, and the broad expanse of valley opening away to the south is just lighting up in chill, half-reluctant fashion, as though the night had been far too short or the revels of yester-even far too long. There is a swish and plash of rapid running waters close at hand, and here and there, where the stream is dammed by rocky ridge, the wisps of fog rise slowly into air, mingling with and adding to the prevailing tone of chilly gray. Through these fog-wreaths there stands revealed a massive barrier of wooded and rock-ribbed heights, towering aloft and shutting out the eastern sky, all their crests a-swim in floating cloud, all their rugged foothills dotted with the tentage of a sleeping army. Here, close at hand on the banks of the rushing river, a sentry paces slowly to and fro, the dew dripping from his shouldered musket and beading on his cartridge-box. The collar of his light-blue overcoat is muffled up about his ears, and his forage cap is

C*

pulled far down over his blinking eyes. As he paces southward he can see along the stream-bed camps and pale-blue ghosts of sentries pacing as wearily as himself in the wan and cheerless light. Trees are dripping with heavy charge of moisture that the faintest whiff of morning air sends showering on the bank beneath; and a little deluge of the kind coming suddenly down upon this particular sentry as he strolls under the spreading branches serves to augment the expression of general weariness and disgust, which by no means distinguishes him from his more distant fellows, but evokes no further comment than a momentary huddling of head and shoulders into the depths of the blue collar, and the briefest possible mention of the last place of all others one would be apt to connect with cooling showers. Facing about and slouching along the other way the sentry sees a picture that, had he poetry or love of the grand and beautiful in his soul, would a thousand-fold compensate him for his enforced vigil. Every moment, as the timid light grows bolder with its reinforcement from the east, there opens a vista before his eyes that few men could look upon unmoved. To his right the brawling Shenandoah, swift and swirling, goes rushing through its last rapids, as though bent on having one final "hurrah" on its own account before losing its identity in the welcoming waters of the Potomac. Hemming it in to the right— the east—and shutting out the crimson dawn are the massive bulwarks of the Loudon Heights climbing towards the changing heavens. Westward, less bold and jagged, but still a mighty barrier in almost any other companionship, are the sister heights of Bolivar, scarred and seamed with earth-work and rifle-pit, and bristling with abattis and battery. Down the intervening valley plunges the Shenandoah and winds the macadam of the highway, its dust subdued for the time being; while, straight away to the front, mistwreathed at their base from the sleeping waters of the winding canal, cloud-capped at their lofty summit from the bank of vapor that hovers along the entire range, rock-ribbed, precipitous, magnificent in silent, stubborn strength, the towering heights of Maryland span the scene from east to west, and stand superb, the background to the picture. All as yet is sombre in tone, black, dark green, and brown and gray. The mist hangs heavy over everything, and the twinkle of an occasional camp-fire is but the sodden

glow of ember whose life is long since burned out.
But, see! Through the deep, jagged rift where
runs the Potomac, along the rock-bound gorge
through which in ages past the torrent burst its
way, there creeps a host of tiny shafts of color—
the skirmishers, the *éclaireurs*, of the irresistible
array of which they form but the foremost line
—the coming army of the God of Day. Here
behind the frowning Loudon no such light troops
venture; but, skilled riders as they are,

"Spurring the winds of the morning,"

they pour through the rocky gap, and now they
find their lodgment on every salient of the grim
old wall beyond the broad Potomac. Here, there,
everywhere along the southern face are glinting
shafts or points on rocks or ridge. Seam and
shadow take on a purplish tinge. The hanging
mass of cloud beams with answering smile upon
its earthward face as gold and crimson and roy-
al purple mantle the billowy cheeks. Now the
rocks light up with warmer glow, and long, hori-
zontal shadows are thrown across the hoary cur-
tain, and slowly the gorgeous cloud-crests lift
away and more and more the heights come
gleaming into view. Now there are breaks and

caverns here and there through the shifting
vapors, and hurried little glimpses of the cliffs
beyond, and these cloud-caves grow and widen,
and broad sheets of yellow light seem warming
up the dripping wall and changing into mist the
clinging beads of dew. And now, far aloft, the
fringe of firs and stunted oaks is seen upon the
summit as the sun breaks through the shimmer-
ing veil, and there, fluttering against the blue of
heaven, circled in fleecy frame of vapor, glowing,
waving in the sky, all aflame with tingeing sunshine, there leaps into view the "Flag of the Free,"
crowning the Maryland heights and shining far
up the guarded valley of the Shenandoah. A
puff of smoke juts out from the very summit
across the stream; the sentry eyes it with a sigh
of reviving interest in life; five, ten, twenty sec-
onds he counts before the boom of the salute
follows the sudden flash and wakes the echoes of
the opposite cliffs.

Listen! Up on the westward heights, somewhere among those frowning batteries, a bugle
rings out upon the air—

"I can't get 'em up, I can't get 'em up,
I can't get 'em up in the mo—orning,"

it merrily sings, and the rocks of Loudon echo

back the spirited notes. Farther up the valley a distant drum rattles, and then, shrill and piercing, with hoarse, rolling accompaniment, the fifes of some infantry regiment burst into the lively trills of the *reveille*. Another camp takes up the strain, off to the left. Then the soft notes of the cavalry trumpets come floating up from the waterside, and soon, regiment after regiment, the field-music is all astir and the melody of the initial effort becomes one ringing, blaring, but most effectually waking discord. Loud in the nearest camp the little drummers and fifers are thumping away at "Bonnie Lass o' Gawrie." Over by the turnpike the rival corps of the —th Connecticut are pounding out the cheerful strains in which Ireland's favored bard declared he would "Mourn the hopes that leave," little dreaming that British fifes and drums would make it soldier music —"two-four time"—all the world over. Halfway across the valley, where the Bolivars narrow it, an Ohio regiment is announcing to the rest of the army, within earshot, that it wakes to the realization that its "Name it is Joe Bowers," tooted and hammered in "six-eight time" through the lines of " A " tents; and a New York Zouave organization turns out of its dew-dripping blank-

ets and cordially blasphemes the musicians who
are expressing as their conception of the regimental sentiment, " Oh, Willie, we have missed
you." And so the chorus goes up and down
the Shenandoah, and the time-worn melodies
of the earliest war-days — the days before we
had " Tramp, tramp," and " Marching through
Georgia" (which we never *did* have in Virginia),
and even lackadaisical " When this crew-el war
is o-ver," are the matins of the soldiers of the
Union Army.

At last the uproar dies away. Here in the
neighboring camp the sergeants are rapidly calling the rolls, and some companies are so reduced
in number that no call over is necessary — a simple glance at the baker's dozen of war-worn, grisly
looking men is sufficient to assure the sergeant of
the presence of every one left to be accounted for.
In this brigade they are not turning out under
arms just now, as is the custom farther to the
front. It has been cruelly punished in the late
battle, and is accorded a resting-spell pending the
arrival of recruits from home. One first sergeant,
who still wears the chevrons of a corporal, in
making his report to his company commander
briefly says:

"Rix came back last night, sir; returned to duty with his company."

"Hello, Hunnewell!" sings out the officer addressed, calling to the new adjutant, who is hurriedly passing by. "What does this mean? Are the wagons back?"

"No," says the adjutant, halting short with the willingness of a man who has news to tell. "Some of the provost-marshal's men came up last night from Point of Rocks and fetched Rix with them, and letters from the colonel. Both he and Abbot made complaint of the man's conduct, and had him relieved and sent up here under guard. Heard about Abbot?"

"No—what?"

"He's appointed major and assistant adjutant-general, and goes to staff duty; and the colonel will be back this week."

"Does he say who's to be quartermaster?" asks the lieutenant with eager interest, and forgetting to record his congratulations on the good-fortune that has befallen his regimental comrade.

"No," says Mr. Hunnewell, with some hesitancy. "There's a hitch there. To begin with, does anybody know that a vacancy exists?"

"Why, Hollins has been missing now ever

since the 18th of September, and he must be either dead or taken prisoner."

The adjutant looks around him, and, seeing other officers and men within earshot, though generally occupied with their morning ablutions, he comes closer to his comrade of the line and the two who have joined him, and speaks with lowered voice.

"There is some investigation going on. The colonel sent for such books and papers of Hollins's as could be found about camp, and an order came last night for Captain Dodge to report at once at Frederick. He was better acquainted with Hollins than any one else—among the officers anyway—and he knew something about his whereabouts the other times he was missing. This makes the third."

"Three times and out, say I," answers one of the party. "I heard some talk at division head-quarters when I was up there last night: the general has a letter that Colonel Raymond wrote soon after he was exchanged, but if it be anything to Hollins's discredit I wonder he did not write to Putnam. He wouldn't want his successor to be burdened with a quartermaster whom he knew to be—well—shady, so to speak."

"That's the one thing I never understood about Abbot," says the captain, sipping the cup of coffee that a negro servant had just brought to him. "Some more of that, Belshazzar; these gentlemen will join me. How he, who is so blue-blooded, seems to be on such terms of intimacy with Hollins is what I mean," he explains. "It was through him that Hollins was taken into companionship from the very start. He really is responsible for him. They were classmates, and no one else knew anything of him—except vaguely."

"Now there's just where you wrong Abbot, captain," answers Mr. Hunnewell, very promptly, "and I want to hit that nail on the head right here. I thought just as you did, for a while; but got an inkling as to the real state of the case some time ago. It wasn't Abbot who endorsed him at all, except by silence and sufferance, you may say. Hollins was at his tent day and night—always following him up and actually forcing himself upon him; and one night, after Hollins had that first scrape, and came back under a cloud and went to Abbot first thing to intercede with the colonel, I happened to overhear a piece of conversation between them. Abbot was just

as cold and distant as man could possibly be.
He told him plainly that he considered his course
discreditable to the whole regiment, and especially annoying to him, because, said Abbot, 'You
have virtually made me your sponsor with every
man who showed a disposition to repel you.'
Then Hollins made some reply which I did not
fully catch, but Abbot was angry, and anybody
could have heard his answer. He told Hollins
that if it had not been for the relationship to
which he alluded he could not have tolerated
him at all, but that he must not draw on it too
often. Then Hollins came out, and I heard him
muttering to himself. He fawned on Abbot
while he was in the tent, but he was scowling
and gritting his teeth when he left; and I heard
him cursing *sotto voce*, until he suddenly caught
sight of me. Then he was all joviality, and took
me by the arms to tell me how 'Paul, old boy,
has been raking me over the coals. We were
chums, you know, and he thinks a heap of me,
and don't want the home people to know of my
getting on a spree,' was the way he explained it.
Now, if you remember, it was Hollins who was
perpetually alluding to his intimacy with the
Abbots. Paul himself never spoke of it. What

Palfrey once told me in Washington may explain it ; he said that Hollins was distantly related to the Winthrops, and that there was a time when he and Miss Winthrop were quite inseparable— you know what a handsome fellow he was when he first joined us ?"

" Well," answers the captain, with the half-way and reluctant withdrawal of the average man who has made an unjust statement, " it may be as you say, but all the same it was Abbot's tacit endorsement or tolerance that enabled Hollins to hold a place among us as long as he has. If he has been sheltered under the shadow of Abbot's wing, and turns out to be a vagabond, so much the worse for the wing. All the same, I'm glad of Abbot's promotion. Wonder whose staff he goes on ?"

" Lieutenant," says a corporal, saluting the group and addressing his company commander, " Rix says he would like to speak with the major before breakfast. He was for going to head-quarters alone just now, but I told him he must wait until I had seen you."

The lieutenant glances quickly around. There, not ten paces away—his forage cap on the back of his head, his hulking shoulders more bent than ever, hands in his pockets and a scowl on his face—stands, or rather slouches, Rix. He looks unkempt, dirty, determinedly ugly, and very much as though he had been in liquor most of the week, and was sober now only through adverse circumstances over which he had no control.

"What do you want of the major, Rix?" demands the lieutenant, with military directness.

"Well, I *want* him—'n that's enough," says the ex-teamster, with surly, defiant manner, and never changing his attitude. "I want t' know what I'm sent back here for, like a criminal."

"Because you look most damnably like one," says the officer, impulsively, and then, ashamed of having said such a thing to one who is powerless to resent, he tempers the wrath with which he would rebuke the man's insubordination, and, after an instant's pause, speaks more gently.

"Come here, Rix. Stand up like a man and tell me your trouble. If you have been wronged in any way I'll see that you are righted; but recollect what and where you are."

"I'm a man, by God! Good as any of you a year ago; better'n most of you five years ago; an' now I'm ordered about by boys just out of their teens. I'm not under Abbot's orders. Lieutenant Hollins is my officer; he'll fix me all right. Where's *he*, lieutenant? He's the man I want."

"Rix, you will only get into more trouble if you don't mend your manners," says the lieutenant, half agreeing with the muttered comment of a comrade, that the man had better be gagged forthwith, but determined to control his own temper. "As to Lieutenant Hollins, he has not been heard of since Antietam. Nobody knows what's become of him."

The effect of this announcement is startling. Rix turns ghastly white; his bloodshot eyes stare fearfully at his informant, then blink savagely around on one after another of the party. His fingers twitch nervously, and he clutches at his throat."

"Are—are you sure, lieutenant?" he gasps, all his insolence of manner gone.

"Sure, sir. He hasn't been seen or heard of since—"

"Why, my God! He told me back there at Boonsboro' that he would ride right over to camp—time I was going back with the colonel through the Gap."

"Boonsboro'! Why, man, that was several days after the battle that you went back with the colonel's ambulance! Then you've seen him since we have. Where was it?"

But Rix has recovered his wits, such as they are. He has made a damaging admission, and one that places him in a compromising position. He quickly blurts forth a denial.

"No, no! It wasn't then. I misremembered. 'Twas when we went over the first time. He says to me right there at Boonsboro'—"

"You're lying, Rix," interposed the senior officer of the party, who has been an absorbed listener. "You didn't go through Boonsboro' at all, first time over. We followed the other road, and you followed us. It must have been when you went back. Now what did the quartermaster say?"

But Rix sets his jaws firmly, and will tell no more. Twice he is importuned, but to no purpose. Then the captain speaks again.

"We need not disturb the commanding officer until breakfast-time, but there is no doubt in my mind this man can give important evidence. I will take the responsibility. Have Rix placed in charge of the guard at once."

And when the corporal reappears it is with a file of men, armed with their Springfields. Be-

5

tween them Rix is marched away, a scared and haggard-looking man.

For a moment the officers stand in silence, gazing after him. Then the captain speaks.

"That man could tell a story, without deviating a hair's-breadth from the truth, that would astonish the commonwealth of Massachusetts, or I am vastly mistaken in him. Does anybody know his antecedents?"

"He was our first quartermaster-sergeant, that's all I know of him," answers Mr. Hunnewell; "but he was in bad odor with the colonel, I heard, long before Cedar Mountain. He would have 'broken' him if it had not been for Hollins's intercessions."

"I mean his antecedents, before the outbreak of the war, not in the regiment. Where did Hollins get him? *Why* did he get him, and have him made quartermaster-sergeant, and stick to him as he did for months, after everybody else was convinced of his worthlessness? There is something I do not understand in their relations. Do you remember, when we were first camped at Meridian Hill, Hollins and Rix occupied the same tent a few days, and the colonel put a stop to it? Hollins was furious, and tried to raise a point against the colonel. He pointed to the fact that in half the regiments around us the quartermaster was allowed to have his sergeant for a tent-mate if he wanted to; and if Colonel Raymond had any objections, why didn't he say so before they left the state? He had lived with him a whole month in camp there, and the colonel never said a word. I confess that some of us thought that Rix was badly treated when he was ordered to pitch his tent elsewhere, but the colonel never permitted any argument. I heard him tell Hollins that what was permissible while we were simply state troops was not to be considered precedent for his action when they were mustered into the national service. In his regiment, as in the well-disciplined regiments of any state, the officers and enlisted men must live apart."

"But Hollins claimed that Rix was a man of good birth and education, and that he was coaching him for a commission," interposes one of the group.

"That was an afterthought, and had no bearing on the case anyway. I know that in this, as in some other matters, there were many of us who chafed a little at the idea of regular army

D

discipline among us, but we know now the colonel was right. As for Rix, he turned out to be a drunkard before we got within rifle-range of Virginia."

"Yet he was retained as quartermaster-sergeant."

"Because Hollins shielded him and kept him out of the way. I tell you," puts in the captain, testily, "Colonel Raymond would have 'broken' him if he had not been taken at Ball's Bluff. Putnam didn't like to overthrow Raymond's appointee without his full knowledge and consent, and so he hung on till after we got back to Alexandria. Even then Hollins had him detailed as driver on plea that his lame foot would prevent his marching. But Hollins is gone now and Mr. ex-Q. M. Sergeant Rix is safely jugged. Mark my words, gentlemen, he'll be needed when Hollins's papers are overhauled."

"Hullo! What's up now?" suddenly demands the adjutant. "Look at headquarters."

From where they stand the broad highway up the valley is plainly visible for a mile or more, and to the right of the turnpike, on a little rising ground, are pitched the tents of the division commander and his staff. Farther away, among some substantial farm-buildings, are to be seen the cavalrymen of the regular service who are attached, as escort and orderlies, to the head-quarters of the Second Corps, and a dozen of these gentry are plainly visible scurrying about between their little tents and the picket-line, where their horses are tethered. It is evident that the whole troop is hurriedly saddling and that orderlies are riding off beyond the buildings, each with one or more led horses—the "mounts" of the staff. Here, close at hand, among the tents of the Massachusetts men, the soldiers have risen to their feet, and with coffee steaming from the battered tin cup in one hand and bread or bacon clutched in the other they are gazing with in-terest, but no sign of excitement, at the scene of evident action farther to the front. A year ago such signs of preparation at headquarters would have sent the whole regiment in eager rush for its arms and equipments, but it has learned wis-dom with its twelve-month of campaigning. Not a shot has been heard up the valley. It can be no attack there. Yet something unquestionably has happened. Yes, the escort is "leading out." See! far up on the heights, to the west, the men are thronging on the parapets. They have a better view from there of what is going on at Sumner's headquarters. Next, shooting around the building on the low rise to the right front, there comes a staff-officer at rapid gallop. Down the slope he rides, over the low stone wall his charger bears him, and down the turnpike he speeds, heedless of the shouts of inquiry that seem to greet him from the camps that flank the road. Sharp to his right he turns, at a little lane a quarter-mile away, and disappears among the trees. "Going to the cavalry camps," hazards the adjutant, and determines that he had better get over to the major's tent—their temporary commander—and warn him "something's coming." Another minute, quick, pealing, spirited, there rings on the air the sound of a trumpet, and the stirring call of " Boots and saddles!" startles the ear of many a late sleeper among the officers. The sun is not yet shining in the valley; the dew is sparkling on every blade and leaf: but the Second Corps is all astir, and there is a cheer in the cavalry camp that tells of soldierly doings close at hand. A light battery is parked just across the highway, and as the aide reappears, spurring from the lane out into the pike again, the officers see how its young commander has

"*The whole troop is hurriedly saddling.*"

vaulted into saddle and is riding down to inter-
cept him so that not a minute be lost if the guns
are needed. They are. For though the aide
comes by like a shot, he has shouted some quick
words to the captain of the battery, and the latter waves his jaunty forage cap to his expectant
bugler, standing, clarion in hand, by the guard-
fire. "Boots and saddles!" again; and—drivers
and cannoneers—the men drop their tin cups
and plates, and leap for the lines of harness.
Down comes the aide full tilt as before. Captain Lee runs to the roadside and hails him with
familiar shout:

"What's up, Win?"

And gets no further answer than

"Tell you as I come back."

Meantime other aides have been scurrying to
and fro; and far and near, up and down the Shenandoah and out across the valley, where the
morning sunshine triumphs over the barring
Loudon, the same stirring call rings out upon the
air. "Boots and saddles!" everywhere, and nowhere the long-roll or the infantry assembly.

"Back to your breakfast, boys," says a tall
and bearded sergeant. "Whatever it is, it don't
amount to shucks. The infantry isn't called for."

But that it amounts to more than "shucks," despite the footman's epigram, is presently apparent when the staff-officer comes more slowly back, easing his panting horse. The major has by this time turned out, and in boots and overcoat is striding over to the stone wall to get the news.

"What is it, Win?" he asks.

And the aide-de-camp, bending low from the saddle and with grave face, replies,

"Stuart again, by Heaven! He whipped around our right, somewhere near Martinsburg, last night, and is crossing at Williamsport now."

" *What!* Why, we've got three corps over there about Antietam yet."

"Yes; and he'll go around them, just as he did round us, and be up in Pennsylvania to-morrow. Where are your wounded?"

"Some over near Keedysville; the others, those we lost at South Mountain, somewhere near Frederick. The colonel and Abbot were there at last accounts. Why?"

"Because it will be just like him to go clean around us and come down the Monocacy. If he should, they are gone, sure."

IV

Two days after the excitement in Frederick consequent upon the escape of the supposed spy Colonel Putnam was chatting with the provost-marshal and the landlord of the tavern where Doctor Warren had paid his brief visit. They were discussing a piece of news that had come in during the morning. From the very first the proprietor of the old tavern had scoffed at the theory of there being anything of a Southern spy about the mysterious stranger. He was a Southern man himself, and, though hardly an enemy to the Union, he had that personal sympathy for a host of neighbors and friends which gave him something of a leaning that way. He did not believe, he openly said, that anything on earth could whip the South so long as they kept on their own soil; but things looked black for their cause when they crossed the Potomac. Maryland had not risen in tumultuous welcome as Lee hopefully expected. The worn, ragged, half-starved soldiers that had marched up the valley in mid-September had little of the heroic in their appearance, despite the fame of their exploits; and in their hunger and thirst they had made way, soldier-fashion, with provender for which they could not pay. The host himself had suffered not a little from their forays, and while his sentiments were broadly Southern his business instincts were emphatically on the side of the greenbacks of the North. He had found the Union officers men of means, if not of such picturesquely martial attributes as their Southern opponents; and while he would not deny his friendship for many a gallant fellow in the rebel gray, neither would he rebuff the blue-coat whose palm was tinged with green. He liked the provost-marshal because that functionary had twice rescued his bar from demolition at the hands of a gang of stragglers. He admired Colonel Putnam as a soldier and a gentleman, but he was enjoying a triumph over both of them; he had news to tell which seemed to sustain his theory and defeat theirs as to the identity of the man who left his beard behind him.

"I am told you knew this Doctor Warren, colonel," he was saying, "and up to this time I had not spoken of him for reasons which—well, because he had reasons for asking me to make no mention of his being here. Now, if he was a Doctor Warren, from the North, and a loyal man, what would he be doing with a spy?"

"I did not know he saw him at all," said Colonel Putnam, quickly.

"Nor do I; but I do believe that he was here purposely to meet him; that he, the man you tried to arrest, was here at this house to meet your friend who followed you out to camp. If Doctor Warren is a loyal man, as you doubtless believe him, he would have no call to be here to get papers from a man who could only meet him in disguise. I'm told the doctor made himself all clear to you as to who he was."

Colonel Putnam's face is a study. He is unquestionably turning pale, and his eyes are filled with a strange, introspective, puzzled look. He is startled, too.

"Do you mean to tell me he *did* have communication with the doctor?" he asks.

"My wife is ready to swear to it," replies mine host. "Her story is simply this: She had come down-stairs just as the doctor returned. She had been sitting with the young lady, who was very

D*

nervous and ill at ease while he was away, and had gone into the kitchen at the back of the house to get her a cup of tea. She was startled by a rap at the door, and in walks a man wrapped up in a big military cape. He wore spectacles and a full black beard, and he took off his hat, and spoke like a gentleman. He said he desired to see either Doctor Warren or the young lady at once on business of the utmost importance, and asked her if she would conduct him up by a rear stairway. My wife told him to go around to the office, but he replied that he expected that, and hastened to tell her that it was because there were Union officers in the hallway that he could not go there. There were personal reasons why he must not be seen; and she said to him that a man who looked like an officer and spoke like a gentleman ought not to be afraid to go among his fellows; and he said he was not an officer, and then asked her, suddenly, if she was a friend to the North or the South; and before she could answer they both saw lights dancing about out there in the yard, and he was startled, and said 'twas for him they were searching, and begged her, as she was a woman, not to betray him; he was the young lady's lover, he said in explanation, and had risked much to meet her. And my wife's heart was touched at that, and she showed him a place to hide; and when she went up she heard the young lady sobbing and the old man trying hard to comfort her; and she knocked, but they begged to be left undisturbed until they called, and she went down and told the man; and he was fearfully nervous and worried, she said, especially when told about the crying going on; and he wrote a few lines on a scrap of paper, gave it to her with a little packet, and she took them up to the doctor; and they were just coming out of their room at the moment, and the doctor put the papers in his pocket, and said to her and to me that he begged us to make no mention of his daughter's being there to any one— there were reasons. And her face was hidden in her veil, and he seemed all broken down with anxiety or illness, and said they must have a carriage or something to take them at once to the railway. They probably went back to Baltimore that night, but the doctor took the packet in his pocket; and the man whom you saw come up from under the back piazza, colonel, was the man who sent it him."

The provost-marshal is deeply interested. Colonel Putnam sits, in a maze of perplexity, silent and astounded.

"The doctor was well known to you, was he not, Putnam?" asked the marshal.

The colonel starts, embarrassed and troubled.

"No. I never saw him before."

"He brought letters to you, didn't he?"

"No letters. In fact, it wasn't me whom he came to see at all."

"Whom did he want, then?"

"Mr. Abbot," answers the colonel, briefly, and with growing embarrassment.

"Oh! Abbot knew him, did he?"

"No; he didn't. That is the singular part of it. The more I recall the interview the more I'm upset."

"Why so?"

"Because he said he had come to see an old friend of his son's whom he mourned as killed at Seven Pines. He named Abbot, and said he had been in correspondence with him for a year. As luck would have it, Abbot was sitting right there beside me, and I said at once, 'Here's your man,' or something like it; and then Abbot didn't know him at all; declared he had never written a line to him; never heard of him. The old gentleman was completely floored. He vowed that for a whole year he had been receiving letters from Lieutenant Paul Revere Abbot, and now had come to see him because he was reported severely wounded."

" Did he show you any of the letters ?"

" Why, no! He said there were none with him. He— I declare I do not know what excuse he *did* give," says the colonel, in dire distress of mind.

The provost-marshal's eyes are glittering, and his face is set and eager. He thinks intently one moment, and then turns on the silent colonel and their perplexed landlord.

" Keep this thing perfectly quiet, gentlemen; I may have to look further into it; but at this moment, colonel, circumstances point significantly at your friend, the doctor. Do you see nothing suspicious in his conduct? His confident claim of a year's correspondence with an officer of your regiment was possibly to gain your friendship and protection. As ill-luck for him and good-luck for us would have it, he named the wrong man. Abbot was there, and could deny it on the spot. The old man was floored, of course; but his only way of carrying the thing through was to play the martyr, and tell the story that for a year somebody had been writing to him daily or weekly over the name of Abbot. What a very improbable yarn, Putnam! Just think for yourself. What man would be apt to do that sort of thing? What object could he have? Why, the doctor himself well realized what a transparent fiction it must appear, and away he slips by the night train the moment he gets back. And now our friend, the landlord, throws further light upon the matter. He was here to meet that night visitor, perhaps convey valuable information to him, but was frightened by the blunder he had made, and got away as speedily as possible, and without seeing the owner of the beard, although a packet of papers was duly handed to him from that mysterious party. Doctor Warren may turn out a candidate for the fortress of that name in your own harbor, colonel."

And, thinking it all over, Putnam cannot make up his mind what to say. There is something in his impression of the doctor that utterly sets at naught any belief that he was acting a part. He was so simple, so direct, so genuine in his manner and in his distress. On the other hand, analyzing the situation, the colonel is compelled to realize that to any one but himself the doctor's story would appear unworthy of credence. He is in this uncomfortable frame of mind when a staff-officer comes to see him with some papers from the quartermaster-general that call for an immediate investigation of the affairs of the missing Lieutenant Hollins, and for two or three days Colonel Putnam is away at the supply depot on the railway. It is there that he learns the pleasant news that his gallant young comrade has been promoted to a most desirable staff position, and ordered to report for duty in Washington as soon as able to travel. He writes a line of congratulation to Abbot, and begs him to be sure and send word when he will come through, so that they may meet, and then returns to his patient overhauling of the garbled accounts of the quondam quartermaster.

No answer comes from Abbot, and the colonel is so busy that he thinks little of it. The investigation is giving him a world of insight into the crookedness of the late administration, and has put him in possession of facts and given rise to theories that are of unusual interest, and so, when he hears that Abbot was able to leave the hospi-

6

tal and ride slowly in to the railway and so on
to Baltimore, he merely regrets not having seen
him, and thinks little of it.

But the provost-marshal has been busily at
work; has interviewed Abbot and cross-exam-
ined the landlady. He has found an officer who
says that the night of the escapade at Frederick
his horse was taken from in front of the house
of some friends he was visiting in the southern
edge of the town, and was found next morning
by the pickets clear down at the bridge where
the canal crosses the Monocacy; and the pickets
said he looked as though he had been ridden hard
and fast, and that no trace of rider could be
found. Inquiry among patrols and guards de-
velops the fact that a man riding such a horse,
wearing such a hat and cape as was described,
but with a smooth face and spectacles, had passed
south during the night, and claimed to be on his
way to Point of Rocks with despatches for the
commanding officer from General Franklin. He
exhibited an order made out for Captain Hol-
lister, and signed by Seth Williams, adjutant-
general of the army in the field. No such officer
had reached Point of Rocks, and the provost-
marshal becomes satisfied that on or about the

4th or 5th of October this very party who was prowling about the town of Frederick has gotten back into Virginia, possibly with valuable information.

When, on the evening of the 10th, there comes the startling news that "Jeb" Stuart, with all his daring gray raiders at his back, has leaped the Potomac at Williamsport, and is galloping up the Cumberland Valley around McClellan's right, the provost-marshal is convinced that the bold dash is all due to information picked up under his very nose in the valley of the Monocacy. If he ever had the faintest doubt of the justice of his suspicions as to "Doctor Warren's" complicity, the doubt has been removed. Already, at his instance, a secret-service agent has visited Hastings, and wires back the important news that the doctor left there about the 25th of September, and has not returned. On the 11th he is rejoiced by a telegram from Washington which tells him that, acting on his advices, Doctor Warren had been found, and is now under close surveillance at Willard's.

Then it is time for him to look out for his own movements. Having leaped into the Union lines with all his native grace and audacity, the cavalier Stuart reposes a few days at Chambersburg, placidly surveying the neighborhood and inviting attack. Then he rides eastward over the South Mountain, and the next heard of him he is coming down the Monocacy. McClellan's army is encamped about Sharpsburg and Harper's Ferry. He has but few cavalry, and, at this stage of the war, none that can compete successfully with Stuart. Not knowing just what to do against so active and calmly audacious an opponent, the Union general is possibly too glad to get rid of him to attempt any check. To the vast indignation and disappointment of many young and ardent soldiers in our lines, he is apparently riding homeward unmolested, picking up such supplies as he desires, paroling such prisoners as he does not want to burden himself with, and exchanging laughing greetings with old friends he meets everywhere along the Monocacy. At Point of Rocks, whither our provost-marshal and Colonel Putnam are driven for shelter, together with numerous squads of convalescents and some dozen stragglers, there is arming for defence, and every intention of giving Jeb a sharp fight should he attempt to pick up supplies or stragglers from its sturdy garrison. Every hour there is exciting news of his coming, and, with their glasses, the officers can see clouds of dust rising high in air far up the valley. Putnam has urgent reason for wanting to rejoin his regiment at once. What with the information he has received from the two or three officers whom he has questioned, and the papers themselves, he has immediate need of seeing the ex-quartermaster sergeant, Rix. But he cannot go when there is a chance for a fight right here. Stuart may dash in westward, and have just one lively tussle with them to cover the crossing of his valuable plunder and prisoners below. Of course they have not men enough to think of confronting him. Just in the midst of all the excitement there comes an orderly with despatches and letters from up the river, and one of them is for Putnam, from the major commanding the regiment. It is brief enough, but exasperating. " I greatly regret to have to report to you, in answer to your directions with regard to Rix, that they came too late. In some utterly unaccountable way, though we fear through collusion on part of a member or members of the guard, Rix made his escape two nights ago, and is now at large."

V.

To say that Paul Abbot was made very happy over his most unexpected promotion would be putting it mildly. He hates to leave the old regiment, but he has done hard fighting, borne several hard knocks, is still weak and shaky from recent wounds; and to be summoned to Washington, there to meet his proud father, and to receive his appointment as assistant adjutant-general from the hands of the most distinguished representative "in Congress assembled" of his distinguished state, is something to put new life into a young soldier's heart. Duties for him there are none at the moment: he is to get strong and well before again taking the field, and, for the time being, he is occupying a room at Willard's adjoining that of his father. His arm is still in a sling; his walk is still slow and somewhat painful; he has ordered his new uniform, and meantime has procured the staff shoulder-straps and buttons, and put them on his sack-

coat; he has had many letters to write, and much
pleasant congratulation and compliment to ac-
knowledge; and so the three or four days succeeding his arrival pass rapidly by. One afternoon he returns from a drive with his father;
they have been out to visit friends in camp, and
talk over home news, and now he comes somewhat slowly up the stairs of the crowded hotel
to the quiet of the upper corridors. He smiles
to himself at the increasing ease with which he
mounts the brass-bound steps, and is thankful for
the health and elasticity returning to him. He
has just had the obnoxious beard removed, too;
and freshly shaved, except where his blond mustache shades the short upper lip, with returning
color and very bright, clear eyes, the young major of staff is a most presentable-looking youth
as he stops a moment to rest at the top of the
third flight. His undress uniform is decidedly
becoming, and all the more interesting because
of the sling that carries his wounded arm. And
now, after a moment's breathing-spell, he walks
slowly along the carpeted corridor, and turns
into the hall-way leading to his own room. Along
this he goes some twenty paces or more, when
there comes quickly into view from a side gallery

the figure of a tall, slight, and graceful girl. She
has descended some little flight of stairs, for he
could hear the patter of her slippered feet, and
the swish of her skirts before she appeared.
Now, with rapid step she is coming straight towards him, carrying some little glass phials in her
hand. The glare of the afternoon sun is blazing
in the street, and at the window behind her.
Against this glare she is revealed only *en silhou-
ette*. Of her features the young soldier can see
nothing. On the contrary, as he is facing the
light, Major Abbot realizes that every line of his
countenance is open to her gaze. Before he has
time to congratulate himself that recent shaving
and the new straps have made him more pre-
sentable, he is astonished to see the darkly-out-
lined figure halt short: he sees the slender hands
fly up to her face in sudden panic or shock;
crash go the phials in fragments on the floor, and
the young lady, staggering against the wall, is
going too—some stifled exclamation on her lips.

Abbot is quick, even when crippled. He springs
to her side just in time to save. He throws his
left arm around her, and has to hug her close to
prevent her slipping through his clasp—a dead
weight—to the floor. She has fainted away, he

sees at a glance, and, looking about him, he finds
a little alcove close at hand; he knows it well,
for there on the sofa he has spent several restful
hours since his arrival. Thither he promptly
bears her; gently lays her down; quickly opens
the window to give her air; then steps across
the hall for aid. Not a soul is in sight. His
own room is but a few paces away, and thither
he hastens; returns speedily with a goblet of ice-
water in his hand, and a slender flask of cologne
tucked under his arm. Kneeling by the sofa, he
gently turns her face to the light, and sprinkles
it 'with water; then bathes, with cologne, the
white temples and soft, rippling, sunny hair.
How sweet a face it is that lies there, all uncon-
scious, so close to his beating heart! Though
colorless and marble-like, there is beauty in every
feature, and signs of suffering and pain in the
dark circles about the eyes and in the lines at the
corners of the exquisite mouth. Even as he clum-
sily but most assiduously mops with his one available hand and looks vaguely around for feminine
assistance, Major Abbot is conscious of a feeling
of proprietorship and confidence that is as unwarranted, probably, as it is new. 'Tis only a faint,
he is certain. She will come to in a moment, so

why be worried? But then, of course, 'twill be embarrassing and painful to her not to find some sympathetic female face at hand when she does revive; and he looks about him for a bell-rope: none nearer than the room, and he hates to leave her. At last comes a little shivering sigh, a long gasp. Then he holds the goblet to her lips and begs her to sip a little water, and, somehow, she does, and with another moment a pair of lovely eyes has opened, and she is gazing wildly into his."

"Lie still one minute," he murmurs. "You have been faint; I will bring your friends."

But a little hand feebly closes on his wrist. She is trying to speak; her lips are moving, and he bends his handsome head close to hers; perhaps she can tell him whom to summon.

But he starts back, amazed, when the broken, half-intelligible, almost inaudible words reach his ears,

"Paul! Papa—said—you were killed. Oh! he will be so glad!"

And then comes a burst of tears.

Abbot rises to his feet and hurries into the hall. He is bewildered by her words. He feels that it must be some case of mistaken identity,

" 'Then bathes, with cologne, the white temples and soft, rippling, sunny hair.' "

but—how strange a coincidence! Close by the fragments of the phials he finds a door key and the presumable number of her room. Only ten steps away from the little flight of stairs he finds a corresponding door, and, next, an open room. Looking therein, he sees a gentle, matronly woman seated by a bedside, slowly fanning some recumbent invalid. She puts her fingers on her lips, warningly, as she sees the uniform at her door.

"Do not wake him, it is the first sound sleep he has had for days," she says. "Is this the army doctor?"

"No," he whispers, "a young lady has just fainted down in the next corridor. Her room adjoins this. Do you know her?"

"Oh, Heaven! I might have known it. Poor child, she is utterly worn out. This is her father. Will you stay here just a few moments? His son was a soldier, too, and was killed—and so was her lover—and it has nearly killed the poor old gentleman. I'll go at once."

Still puzzling over his strange adventure, and thinking only of the sweet face of the fainting girl, Abbot mechanically takes the fan the nurse has resigned and slowly sweeps the cir-

E

cling flies away. The invalid lies on his right
side with his face to the wall; but the soft, curl-
ing gray hair ripples under the waves of air
stirred by the languid movement of the fan.
The features have not yet attracted his attention.
He is listening intently for sounds from the corridor. His thoughts are with the girl who has
so strangely moved him; so strangely called his
name and looked up into his eyes with a sweet
light of recognition in hers—with a wild thrill of
delight and hope in them, unless all signs deceive
him. The color, too, that was rushing into her
face, the sudden storm of emotion that bursts
in tears; what meant all this—all this in a girl
whom never before had he seen in all his life?
Verily, strange experiences were these he was
going through. Only a week or so before had
not that gray-haired old doctor shown almost as
deep an emotion on meeting him at Frederick?
And was he not prostrated when assured of his
mistake, and was it not hard to convince him
that the letters to which he persistently referred
were forgeries? Some scoundrel who claimed to
know his son was striving to bleed him for money,
probably, and using, of all others, the name of
Paul Abbot. And this poor old gentleman here

had also lost a son, and the sweet, fragile-looking girl a lover! How peacefully the old man sleeps, thinks Abbot, as he glances a moment around the room. There are flowers on the table near the open window; books, too, which, perhaps, she had tried to read aloud. The window opens out over Pennsylvania Avenue, and the hum and bustle of thronging life comes floating up from below; a roar of drums is growing louder every minute, and presently bursts upon the ear as though, just issuing from a neighboring street, the drummers were marching forth upon the avenue. Abbot glances at his patient, fearful lest the noise should wake him, but he sleeps the sleep of exhausted nature, and the soldier in his temporary nurse prompts him to steal to the window and look down upon the troops. They are marching south, along Fourteenth Street—a regiment going over to the fortifications beyond the Long Bridge, and, after a glance, Abbot steps quickly back. On the table nearest the window lies a dainty writing-case, a woman's, and the flap is down on a half-finished letter. On the letter, half disclosed, is the photograph of an officer. It is strangely familiar as Abbot steps towards it. Then—the roar of the drums seems deafening; the walls of the little room seem turning upside down; his brain is in some strange and sudden whirl; but there in his hands he holds, beyond all question—his own picture—a photograph by Brady, taken when he was in Washington during the previous summer. He has not recovered his senses when there is an uneasy movement at the bed. The gray-haired patient turns wearily and throws himself on the other side, and now, though haggard and worn with suffering, there is no forgetting that sorrow-stricken old face. In an instant Major Abbot has recognized his visitor of the week before. There before him lies Doctor Warren. Who—*who* then is *she?*

VI.

SITTING by the open window and looking out over the bustling street Major Abbot later in the evening is trying to collect his senses and convince himself that he really is himself. "It never rains but it pours," and events have been pouring upon him with confusing rapidity. Early in the summer he had noted an odd constraint in the tone of the few letters that came from Miss Winthrop. That they were few and far between was not in itself a matter to give him much discomfort. From boyhood he had been accustomed to the household cry that at some time in the future—the distant future—Viva Winthrop was to be his wife. He had known her quite as long as he had been conscious of his own existence, and the relations between the families were such as to render the alliance desirable. Excellent friends were the young people as they grew to years of discretion, and, in the eyes of parents and intimate acquaintances, no formal betrothal was ever necessary, simply because "it was such an understood thing." For more than a year previous to the outbreak of the war, however, Miss Winthrop was in Europe, and much of the time, it was said, she had been studying. So had Mr. Hollins, who withdrew from Harvard in his second year and read law assiduously in the office of Winthrop & Lawrence, and then went abroad for his health. They returned on the Cunarder in the early part of April, and Mrs. Winthrop was ill from the time she set foot on the saloon deck until they sighted the State House looming through the fog, and nothing could have been more fortunate than that Mr. Hollins was with them—he was so attentive, so very thoughtful. When he wasn't doing something for her he was promenading with Viva on deck or bundling that young lady in warm wraps and hedging her in a sunny corner. Pity that Mr. Hollins was so poor and rather obscure in his family—his immediate family — connections. His mother was Mr. Winthrop's first cousin, and she had been very fond of Mr. Winthrop when she was a child, and he had befriended her son when a friend was needed. She died years ago, and no one knew just when her husband followed her. He was a person no one ever met, said Mrs. Winthrop, a man who had a singular career, was an erratic genius, and very dissipated. But he was a very fascinating person, she understood, in his younger days, and his son was most talented and deserving, but entirely out of the question as an intimate or associate. Viva would not be apt to see anything of him after their return; but the question never seemed to occur to her, how much had the daughter been influenced by their frequent companionship abroad? It really mattered nothing. Viva was to marry Revere Abbot, as Mrs. Winthrop preferred to call him, and such was distinctly the family understanding. Miss Winthrop had been home but a few weeks when all the North was thrilled by the stirring call for volunteers, and the old Bay State responded, as was to be expected of her. In the —th Massachusetts were a score of officers, as has been said, whose names were as old as the colony and whose family connections made them thoroughly well known to each other at the earliest organization of the command. That Paul Abbot should be among the first to seek a commission as a junior lieutenant was naturally expected. Then with all possible hesitancy and

7

delicacy, after a feminine council in the family, his mother asked him if he did not think there ought to be some distinct understanding about Viva Winthrop before he went away to the front. The matter was something that he had thought of before she went to Europe, but believed then that it could wait. Now that she had returned, improved both physically and intellectually, Mr. Abbot had once or twice thought that it would not be long before he would be asked some such question as his mother now propounded, but again decided that it was a matter that could be deferred. They had met with much hearty cordiality, and called each other Paul and Viva, as they had from babyhood, and then she had a round of social duties and he became absorbed in drills, day and night, and they saw very little of each other—much less than was entirely satisfactory to the parental councils, and these were frequent. While the masters of the households of Abbot and Winthrop seldom interchanged a word on the subject, they had their personal views none the less; and, as to the mothers, their hearts had long been set upon the match. Miss Winthrop had abundant wealth in her own right. Paul Abbot's blood was blue as the doctrines of the Puritans. Without being a beauty in face or form, Miss Winthrop was unquestionably distinguished-looking, and her reputation for a certain acerbity of temper and the faculty of saying cutting things did not materially lower her value in the matrimonial market. There was, however, that constantly recurring statement, "Oh, she's engaged to Paul Abbot," and that, presumably, accounted for the lack of those attentions in society which are so intangible when assailed, and yet leave such a void when omitted. Mrs. Abbot put it very plainly to Paul when she said:

"Everybody considers her as virtually engaged to you and expects you to look after her. That is why I say it is due to her that you should arrive at some understanding before your orders come."

Paul had come up from camp that day—a Saturday afternoon—and he stood there in the old family gathering room, a very handsome young soldier. He had listened in silence and respect while his mother spoke, but without much sign of responsive feeling. When she had finished he looked her full in the face and quietly said:

E*

"And is there any other reason, mother?"

Mrs. Abbot flushed. There was another reason, and one that after much mental dodging both she and Mrs. Winthrop had been compelled to admit to each other within a very few days. Mr. Hollins was constantly finding means to come over to the city and see Miss Winthrop, and the ladies could not grapple with the intricacies of a military problem which permitted one officer to be in town three or four days a week and kept the others incessantly drilling at camp. Mrs. Abbot, motherlike, had more than once suggested to her son that he ought to be able to visit town more frequently, and on his replying that it was simply impossible, and that none of the officers could leave their duties, had triumphantly pointed to Mr. Hollins.

"But he is quartermaster," said Paul, "and has to come on business."

"He manages to combine a good deal of pleasure with his business," was the tentative response, and Abbot knew that he was expected to ask the nature of Mr. Hollins's pleasures. He was silent, however, much to his mother's disappointment, for he had heard from other sources of the frequency with which Mr. Hollins and Miss Winthrop were seen together. Finding that he would not ask, Mrs. Abbot was compelled to suppress the inclination she felt to have her suspicions dragged to light. She wished he had more curiosity, or jealousy, or something; but in its absence she could only say,

"Well, I wish you were quartermaster, that's all."

And now that he *had* asked her if there were no other reason, there was something in his placid tone she did not like. A month agone she wanted him to know of Mr. Hollins's evident attentions to Genevieve because it would probably, or possibly, spur him into some exertion on his own account. Now that she felt sure he had heard of it, and it had not spurred him, she was as anxious to conceal the fact that, both to Mrs. Winthrop and herself, these attentions were becoming alarming. If he did *not* care for Viva, the chances were that so soon as he found that public attention had been drawn to her acceptance of such devotions, Paul would drop the matter entirely, and that would be a calamity. Knowing perfectly well, therefore, what was in his mind when he asked the question, Mrs. Abbot parried the thrust. Though she flushed, and her voice quivered a little, she looked him straight in the face.

"There is, Paul. I — think she has a right to expect it of you ; that—that she does expect it."

Abbot looked with undisguised perplexity into his mother's face.

" You surprise me very much, mother; I cannot see how Viva would betray such an idea, even if she had it; it is not like her."

"Women see these things where men cannot," was the somewhat sententious reply. " Besides, Paul—"

" Well, mother, besides—?"

" Mrs. Winthrop has told me as much."

That evening, before returning to camp, Lieutenant Abbot went round the square — or what is the Bostonian equivalent therefor — and surprised Miss Winthrop with a call. He told her what he had not told his mother, that Colonel Raymond that morning received a telegram from Washington saying that on the following Tuesday they must be in readiness to start.

" We have been good friends always, Viva," he said; " but you have been something more to me than that. I did not mean to make so sudden an avowal, but soldiers have no time to call their own just now, and every hour has been given up to duty with the regiment. Now this sharp summons comes and I must go. If I return, shall we—" (he had almost said, "shall we fulfil our manifest destiny, and make our parents happy?" but had sense enough to realize that she was entitled to a far more personal proposition). He broke off nervously.

"You have always been so dear to me, Viva. Will you be my wife?"

She was sitting on the sofa, nervously twisting the cords of a fan in and out among her slender white fingers. Her eyes were downcast and her cheeks suffused. For an instant she looked up and a question seemed trembling on her lips. She was a truthful woman and no coward. There was something she was entitled to know, something the heart within her craved to know, yet she knew not how to ask, or, if she did, was too proud to frame the words, to plead for that thing of all others which a woman prizes and glories in, yet will never knowingly beg of any man—his honest and outspoken love. She looked down again, silent.

His tone softened and his voice quivered a little as he bent over her.

"Has any one else won away the heart of my little girl-love?" he asked. "We were sweet-hearts so long, Viva; but have you learned to care for some other?"

"No. It—it is not that."

"Then cannot you find a little love for me left over from the childish days? You were so loyal to me then, Viva—and it would make our home people so happy."

"I suppose it might—them."

"Then promise me, dear; I go so soon, and—"

She interrupted him now, impetuously. Look-ing straight up into his eyes, she spoke in low, vehement tone, rapidly, almost angrily.

"On this condition, Paul; on this condition. You ask me to be your wife and—and I suppose it is what is expected of us — what you have ex-pected all along, and are entitled to an answer now. Promise me this, if ever you have a thought for another woman, if ever you feel in your heart that perhaps another girl would make you hap-pier, or if—if you feel the faintest growing fancy for another, that you will tell me."

He smiled gravely as he encircled her in his arm. She drew back, but he held her.

"Why, Viva, I have never had a thought for

any other girl. I simply thought you might care for some one more than you did for me. It is settled, then — I promise," and he bent and softly kissed her.

They met again—twice—before the regiment took the cars. It had been settled that no announcement of the engagement should be made, but there are some secrets mothers cannot keep, and there were not lacking men and women to obtrude premature "congratulations" even on the day she came with mothers, sisters, cousins, and sweethearts by the score to witness the presentation of colors and say adieu. That afternoon the regimental quartermaster returned from the city after a stay of thirty-six hours, thirty of which were unauthorized, and it was rumored that Colonel Raymond was very angry and had threatened extreme measures. It was this prospect, possibly, that shrouded Mr. Hollins's face in gloom, but most people were disposed to think that he had taken the engagement very much to heart. There were many who considered that, despite the fact of his lack of fortune, birth, and "position," Mr. Hollins had been treated very shabbily by the heiress. There were a few who said that but for his "lacks" she would have married him. What she herself said was something that caused Mr. Abbot a good deal of wonderment and reflection.

"Paul, I want you to promise me another thing. Mr. Hollins has very few friends in the regiment. He is poor, sensitive, and he feels it keenly. He is our kinsman, though distant, and he placed me under obligations abroad by his devotion to mother, and his courtesy to me when we needed attention. He thinks you dislike him, as well as many of the others. Remember what he is to us, and how hard a struggle he has had, and be kind to him—for me."

And though his college remembrances of Mr. Hollins were not tinged with romance, Paul Abbot was too glad and proud in the thought of going to the front—too happy and prosperous, perhaps, to feel anything but pity for the quartermaster's isolation. He made the promise, and found its fulfilment, before they had been away a fortnight, a very irksome thing. Hollins fairly lived at his tent and better men kept away. Gradually they had drifted apart. Gradually the feeling of coldness and aversion had become so marked that he could not conceal it; and finally, after one of the frequent lapses of which the quartermaster was guilty, there had come rupture of all social relations, and the only associate left to Mr. Hollins was the strange character whom he had foisted upon the regiment at its organization — the quondam quartermaster-sergeant, Rix.

But in all the marching and fighting of the battle summer of '62, these things were of less account than they had been during the inaction of the winter and early spring, until, at the Monocacy, Mr. Abbot's curiosity was excited by the singular language used by Rix when ordered under guard. What could such a man as he have to do with the affairs, personal or professional, of the officers of the regiment? It was rabid nonsense—idle boasting, no doubt; and yet the new-made major found that melodramatic threat recurring to his mind time and again.

Another thing that perplexed him was the fact already alluded to, that during the winter Viva's letters, never too frequent or long, had begun to grow longer as to interval and shorter as to contents. He made occasional reference to the fact, but was referred to the singular circumstance that " he began it." Matters were mended for a while, then drifted into the old

channel again. Then came the stirring incidents of June; the sharp, hard marches of July
and August; the thrilling battles of Cedar Mountain and Second Bull Run; and he felt that his
letters were hardly missed. Then came the dash
at Turner's Gap; his wounds, rest, recovery, and
promotion. But there was silence at home. He
had not missed *her* letters before. Now he felt
that they ought to come, and had written more
than once to say so.

And now, alone in his room, he is trying to
keep cool and clear-headed; to fathom the mystery of his predicament before going to his father
and telling him that between Genevieve Winthrop and himself there has arisen a cloud which
at any moment may burst in storm.

Her letter—the first received since Antietam—
he has read over time and again. It must be
confessed that there is a good deal therein to
anger an honest man, and Abbot believes he is
entitled to that distinction:

"You demand the reason for my silence, and shall have
it. I did not wish to endanger your recovery, and so have
kept my trouble to myself, but now I write to tell you that
the farce is ended. You have utterly broken your promise;
I am absolved from mine. The fact that you could find time

to write day after day to Miss Warren, and neglect me for weeks, would in itself be justification for demanding my release from an engagement you have held so lightly. But that you should have sought and won another's love even while your honor was pledged to me, is *more* than enough. I do not ask release. I break the bond—once and for all.

"You will have no place to receive your letters at the front. They, with your ring, and certain gifts with which you have honored me from time to time, will be found in a packet which is this day forwarded to your mother.

"GENEVIEVE WINTHROP."

Abbot is seated with his head buried in his hands. That name again! the girl who fainted at sight of him! the old man who was prostrate at his denial on the Monocacy! the picture of himself in *her* desk! and now, this bitter, insulting letter from the woman who was to have been his wife! Rix's words at the field hospital!—what in Heaven's name can it all mean? What network of crime and mystery is this that is thrown around him?

There is a sudden knock at the door—a negro waiter with a telegram:

"POINT OF ROCKS, MD., *Oct.* —, 1862.

"Major PAUL R. ABBOT,

Willard's Hotel, Washington:

"Hollins still missing; believed to have followed you to Washington. Use every effort to secure arrest.

"PUTNAM."

VII.

THERE is an air of unusual excitement about the War Department this bright October day. It is only a month since the whole army seemed tramping through the streets on its way to the field of the Antietam; only three weeks since the news was received that Lee was beaten back across the Potomac, and every one expected that McClellan would be hot on his trail, eager to pursue and punish before the daring Southerners could receive accessions. But though two corps managed to reoccupy Harper's Ferry and there go into camp, the bulk of the army has remained where Lee left it when he slipped from its grasp, and McClellan's cry is for reinforcements. Three weeks of precious time slip by, and then—back come those daredevils of Stuart's, riding with laugh and taunt and jeer all around the Union forces; and there is the mischief to pay here in Washington, for if he should take a notion to pay the capital a visit on his homeward trip, what

" Back come those daredevils of Stuart's."

would the consequences be? Of course there are troops—lots of them—all around in the fortifications. The trouble is, that we have so few cavalry, and, after all, the greatest trouble is the old one—those fellows, Stuart and Jackson, have such a consummate faculty of making a very little go a great way. All that is known of Stuart's present move is, that he is somewhere up the Cumberland Valley; that telegraphic communication beyond McClellan's headquarters is broken, and that it is more than likely he will come hitherwards when he chooses to make his next start.

Going to the War Department to make inquiries for the provost-marshal, and show him Putnam's telegram, Major Abbot finds that official too busy to see him, "unless it be something urgent," says the subaltern, who seems to be an aide-de-camp of some kind.

"I have come to show him a despatch received last night—late—from Point of Rocks."

"You are Major Abbot, formerly —th Massachusetts, I believe, and your despatch is about the missing quartermaster, is it not?"

"Yes," replies Abbot, in surprise.

"We have the duplicate of the despatch here,"

says the young officer, smiling. "You would know Hollins at once, would you not?"

"Yes, anywhere, I think."

"One of the secret-service men will come in to see you this morning if you will kindly remain at your room until eleven or twelve o'clock. Pardon me, major, you saw this Doctor Warren at Frederick, did you not?"

"Yes. The evening he came out to the field hospital."

"Did he impress you as a man who told a perfectly straight story, and properly accounted for himself?"

"Why— You put it in a way that never occurred to me before," says the major, in bewilderment. "Do you mean that there was anything wrong about him?"

"Strictly *entre nous*, major—something damnably wrong. He was all mixed up on meeting you, we are told. He claimed to have known and been in correspondence with you, did he not?"

"Yes; he did. But—"

"That is only one of several trips he made. There are extraordinary rumors coming in about spies around Frederick, and there seems to be an organized gang. It is this very matter the general is overhauling now, and he gave orders that he should be uninterrupted until he had finished the correspondence. Will you wait?"

"Thank you, no. I believed it my duty to show him this despatch, but he knows as much as, or more than, I do. May I ask if you have any inkling of Hollins's whereabouts."

"Not even a suspicion. He simply dropped out of sight, and no man in the army appears to have set eyes on him since the night before Antietam. Colonel Putnam is investigating his accounts at Point of Rocks, and is most eager to get him."

Major Abbot turns away with a heavy weight at heart. All of a sudden there has burst upon him a complication of injustice and mystery, of annoyance and perplexity that is hard to bear. In some way he feels that the disappearance of the quartermaster is a connecting link in the chain of circumstance. He associates him, vaguely, with each and every one of the incidents which have puzzled him within the month past—with Rix, with Doctor Warren's coming, with that cold and bitter letter from Miss Winthrop, and finally with the shock and faintness that overcame this fair young girl at sight of him.

8

To his father he has shown Miss Winthrop's letter, and briefly sketched the visit of Doctor Warren, and the sudden meeting with his daughter the evening previous. Mr. Abbot is in a whirl of indignation over the letter, which he considers an insult, but is all aflame with curiosity about the doctor and the young lady. He has been preparing to return to Boston this very week, but is now determined to wait until he can see these mysterious people, who are so oddly mixed up in his son's affairs. It is with some difficulty that the major prevails upon him not to write to Miss Winthrop, and overwhelm her with reproaches. That letter must be answered only by the man to whom it was written, says Abbot, and it is evident that he does not mean to be precipitate. He has much to think of, and so drives back to Willard's and betakes himself to his room, where his father awaits him, and where they are speedily joined by an official of the secret service, who has a host of singular questions to ask about Hollins. Some of them have a tendency to make the young major wonder if he really has been the possessor of eyes and ears, or powers of discernment, during the past winter. Then come some inquiries about

Rix. Abbot is forced to confess that he knows nothing of his antecedents, and that he was made quartermaster-sergeant at Hollins's request, at a time when nobody had a very adequate idea of what his duties might be.

"Who had charge of the distribution of the regimental mail all winter and spring?" asks the secret-service man, after looking over some memoranda.

"The quartermaster, ordinarily. The mail-bag was carried to and from the railway about thrice a week, while we were at Edward's Ferry in the fall. Rix looked after it then, and when we came down in front of Washington the matter still remained in his hands. There was never any complaint, that I can remember."

"Did any of your officers besides Mr. Hollins have civilian dress or disguise of any kind?"

"I did not know that he did—much less any of the others."

"He wore his uniform coming to the city, but would soon turn out in 'cits,' and in that way avoided all question from patrols. As he gambled and drank a good deal then, we thought, perhaps, it was a rule in the regiment that officers must not wear their uniforms when on a lark of any kind; but he was always alone, and seemed to have no associates among the officers. What use could he have had for false beard and wig?"

"None whatever that I know of."

"He bought them here, as we know, and, presumably, took them down to camp with him. If he has deserted, he is probably masquerading in that rig now. I tell you this knowing you will say nothing of it, Major Abbot, and because I feel that you have had no idea of the real character of this man, and it is time you had."

Abbot bows silently. If the detective only knew what was going on at home, how much the more would he deem the missing quartermaster a suspicious character.

Then there comes a knock at the door, and, opening it, Major Abbot finds himself face to face with the nurse whom he had seen the previous afternoon in Doctor Warren's room. She looks up into his face with a smile that betokens a new and lively interest.

"The doctor left us but a few minutes ago," she says, "and he tells me my patient is on the mend. Of course, we have said nothing to him as yet about Miss Bessie's fainting yesterday, but—I thought you might be anxious to know how they are."

"I am indeed," says Abbot, cordially, "and thank you for coming. How is Miss Warren to-day?"

"She keeps her room, as is natural after one has been so agitated, and, of course, she does not like to speak of the matter, and has forbidden my telling the doctor—her father, I mean. But he will be sitting up to-morrow, probably, and—I thought you might like to see them. He is sleeping quietly now."

"Yes, I want very much to see him, as soon as he is well enough to talk, and, if the young lady should be well enough to come out into the parlor this afternoon or take the air on the piazza, will you let me know?"

The nurse's smiles of assent are beaming. Whether she, too, has seen that photograph Abbot cannot tell. That she has had the feminine keenness of vision in sighting a possible romance is beyond question. The secret-service official is at Abbot's side as he turns back from the door.

"I shall see you again, perhaps to-morrow," he says; "meantime there is a good deal for us to do," and before the nurse has reached the sick man's door, she is politely accosted by the same urbane young man, and is by no means sorry to stop and talk with somebody about her sad-faced old patient and his wonderfully pretty daughter.

It was Abbot's purpose to devote a little time that afternoon to answering the letter received but yesterday from Miss Winthrop. It needs no telling—the fact that there had never been a love-affair in their engagement; and no one can greatly blame a woman who is dissatisfied with a loveless match. Viva Winthrop was not so unattractive as to be destitute of all possibility of winning adorers. Indeed, there was strong ground for believing that she fully realized the bliss of having at least one man's entire devotion. Whatsoever evil traits may have cropped out in Mr. Hollins's army career, *she* had seen nothing of them, and knew only his thoughtful and lover-like attentions while they were abroad, and his assiduous wooing on his return. Paul Abbot had never asked for her love—indeed, he had hardly mentioned the word as incidental to their engagement. Nevertheless, yielding to what she had long been taught to consider her fate, she had accepted the family arrangement—and him—and was the subject of incessant and enthusiastic congratulation. Abbot's gallant service and distinguished character as an officer had won the hearty admiration of all the circle in which she lived and moved and had her being, and she was thought an enviable girl to have won the love of so brave and so promising a man. A little more reserved and cold than ever had Miss Winthrop become, and the smile with which she thanked these many well-wishers was something wintry and weary in the last degree. If he had only loved her, there might have bloomed in her heart an answering passion that would have filled her nature, and made her proudly happy in her choice. But that he had never had for her anything more than a brother-and-sister, boy-and-girl sort of affection—a kind, careless, yet courteous tenderness—was something she had to tell herself time and again, and to hear as well from the letters of a man whose letters she should have forbidden.

Even in his astonishment at the charge brought against him, and in his indignation at the accusation of deceit, Paul Abbot cannot but feel that allowances must be made for Viva Winthrop. He meant to marry her, to be a loyal and affectionate husband; but he had not loved her as

women love to be loved, and she was conscious
of the lacking chord. That she had been deceived and swindled, too, by some shameless
scoundrel, and made to believe in her *fiancé's*
guilt, was another thing that was plain to him.
She had probably been told some very strong
story of his interest in this other girl. Very
probably, too, Hollins was the informer and, presumably, the designer of the plot. Who can tell
how deep and damnable it was, since it had been
carried so far as to induce the Warrens to believe
that he was the writer of scores of letters from
the front? Then again, ever since he had raised
that fainting girl in his arms, especially ever
since the moment when her lovely eyes were
lifted to his face and her sweet lips murmured
his name, Paul Abbot has been conscious of a
longing to see her again. Not an instant has he
been able to forget her face, her beauty, her
soft touch; the wave of color that rushed to her
brow as he met her at her father's door when the
nurse brought her, still trembling, back to the old
man's bedside. He had murmured some hardly
articulate words, some promise of coming to inquire for her on the morrow, and bowed his
adieu. But now—now, he feels that not only

Genevieve, but that Bessie Warren, too, has been made a victim of this scoundrel's plottings, and, though longing to see her and hear her speak again, he knows not what to say. It was hard enough to have to deny himself to the poor old doctor when he came out to the Monocacy. *Could* he look in her face and tell her it was all a fraud; that some one had stolen and sent her his picture? some one had stolen and used his name, and, whatsoever were the letters, all were forgeries? No! He must wait and see Doctor Warren, and let her think him come back to life —let her think they *were* his letters—rather than face her, and say it was all a lie. Yet he longs to see her once again.

But to Viva he must write without further delay. Her letter unquestionably frees him, and does it with a brusqueness that might excuse a man for accepting the situation without a word. If the engagement has ever been irksome to him it is now at an end, and he is in no wise responsible. Giving him no opportunity for denial, she has accused him of breach of faith and cast him off. Wounded pride, did he love her deeply, might now impel him to be silent. A sense of indignity and wrong might drive many a man to turn away at such a juncture, and leave to the future the unravelling of the plot. There are moments, it must be confessed, when Major Abbot is so stung by the letter that he is half disposed to take it as final, and let her bear the consequences of discovery of the fraud; but they are quickly followed by others in which he is heartily ashamed of himself for such a thought. Right or wrong, Viva Winthrop is a woman who has given her life into his hands; a woman who has been reared in every luxury only to be denied the one luxury a woman holds most precious of all. He has not been a devoted lover any more than he has been disloyal; and now that trouble has come to her, and she is deceived, perhaps endangered, Major Abbot quietly decides that the only obvious course for a gentleman to follow is to crush his pride under foot and to act and think for her. And this, after several attempts, is what he finally writes her:

"Your letter came last night, dear Viva, and I have thought long over it before answering. It is all my fault that this constraint has hung over your letters. I have seen it for months, and yet made no effort until lately to have it explained. Long ago, had I done so, you would probably have given me the reason, and I could have assured you of the er-

ror into which you were led. Now it seems that you and I
are not the only ones involved.

"Neither to Miss Warren nor any other girl have I written
since our engagement; but her father has been to see me, and
tell me that many letters purporting to come from me have
been received, and I have hardly time to recover from that
surprise when your indignant charge is added. Taken together, the two point very strongly to a piece of villainy.
You could never have believed this of me, Viva, without
proofs; and I feel sure that letters must have been sent to
you. Now that we are pushing every effort to detect and
punish the villain who has wrought this, and I fear other
wrongs, such letters will be most important evidence, and I
conjure you to send them to me by express at once. Father
would come for them, but I need him here. I do not seek to
inquire into your personal correspondence, Viva, but letters
that bear upon this matter are of vital weight.

"As to my dismissal, may I not ask you to reconsider your
words, and, in the light of my assurance that I am innocent
of the sin with which you have charged me, permit me to sign
myself, as ever, lovingly and faithfully yours?   PAUL."

It is no easy letter to write. He wants to
be calm and just, and that makes it sound cold
and utterly unimpassioned. Beyond doubt she
would be far happier with a fury of reproaches,
cutting sarcasm, and page after page of indignant denial. He also wants to be tender when
he thinks of what he has not had to lavish on
her in the past, and that prompts him to the lit-

F*

tle touch of sentiment at the close—a touch that is perhaps unwarranted by the facts in the case. There is a third matter, one that he does not want to mention at all, a name he hates to put on any page addressed to her; but he knows that it is due her she should be told the truth, and at last, just as sunset is coming, he adds a postscript:

"I feel that I must tell you that Mr. Hollins has been missing ever since Antietam, under circumstances that cloud his name with grave suspicion. It is no longer concealed that his conduct and character have left him practically friendless in the regiment, and that he could not long have retained his position. He is not worthy the friendship you felt for him, Viva; of that I am certain."

He is still pondering over this when his father comes in for a word or two.

"I am going over to call at Doctor Warren's room and ask how he is. Possibly he may be able to see me. Have you written to—"

And he stops. He does not feel like saying "Viva" to or of the girl who has so misjudged his boy.

Abbot holds up the letter and its addressed envelope.

"Yes, and it must go at once or miss the mail."

"I'll post it for you, then, as I have to go to

the office a moment," is the answer, and the elder stands looking at his son, while the latter quickly scans the last page, then folds and encloses it. Paul smiles into his father's eyes as he hands it, and the letter-bearer goes briskly away.

His footsteps have hardly become inaudible when there is a tap at the door, and behold! the nurse.

"You told me you would like to know when Miss Warren came out, major. She is on the veranda now."

VIII.

THROWING over his shoulders the cape of his army overcoat, Major Abbot hastens from his room in the direction of the little gallery or veranda at the side of the house. Evening is just approaching, and the lights are beginning to twinkle on the broad avenue below. He has not yet had time to determine upon his course of conduct. If, as he begins to suspect, it is Bessie Warren who received all those guileful letters, his will be a most difficult part to play. He longs to speak with her as well as to see her, but at this moment he knows not what may be expected of him, and, rather than have to inflict mortification or pain upon so sweet a girl, he is almost ready to wish that it had been his privilege to write to her. The fact that her father was so overcome at his denial, the fact that she fainted at sight of him, the fact that her first words on reviving were to the effect that her father had told her Paul Abbot was dead—all seemed to point to the conclusion that she had received love-letters, and that she had become deeply interested in her unseen correspondent. It would be no difficult matter to act the lover, and endorse anything these letters might have said to such a girl, thinks Abbot, as he hastens along the carpeted corridor, but then there is his letter to Viva; there is the fact that he has virtually declined to release her. It is this thought that suddenly "gives him pause," and, at the very moment that he comes to the doorway leading to the veranda, causes him to stop short and reflect.

There is a little sitting-room opening off this hallway. One or two couples are chatting and gossiping therein, but Abbot steps past them to the window and gazes out. As he expected, there is a view of one end of the veranda, and there she stands, looking far out into the gathering night.

A sweeter, lovelier face one seldom sees; so delicate and refined in every feature, so gentle and trusting in its expression. Her deep mourning seems only to enhance her fragile beauty, and to render more observable the grace of her slender form. She leans against the iron trellis-work, and one slim white hand sweeps back the sunny hair that is playing about her temple. Her thoughts are not so very far away. He is standing in the shadow of a curtained niche in a room whose light comes mainly from the flickering coal-fire in the grate, for the October evening is chill. She stands where the light from the big lamps at the corner is sufficient to plainly show her every look and gesture. Abbot marks that twice or thrice, as footsteps are heard in the hall, she glances quickly towards the doorway; then that a shade of disappointment gathers on her brow as no one comes. Then, once or twice, timidly and furtively, she casts shy, quick glances aloft and towards the front of the building. It requires little calculation to tell Major Abbot that those glances are towards the window of his room. Then can it be that she is there, waiting him, impatient of his coming?

Whether or no, this is no place for him. He has no business here spying upon her. He has had his look; has seen again the sweet face that so fascinated him. Now, though he could gaze indefinitely, he feels that he should either go forth and meet her openly or, perhaps better, retire and avoid her entirely. Before he can summon courage to go he turns for one last look, and his course is decided for him.

A footstep, somewhat slow, either from a disposition to saunter on the part of the promenader or possible languor and weakness, is coming along the hallway. She hears it, too, and he sees how her white hands clasp the rail of the balcony, and how she turns her bonnie head to listen. Nearer it comes; he cannot see who approaches, because that would involve his stepping back and losing sight of her; and as it nears the doorway he marks her eager, tremulous pose, and can almost see the beating of her heart. She has not turned fully towards the hall—just partially, as though a sidelong glance were all she dared give even in her joyous eagerness. Then a form suddenly darkens the portal, and just as suddenly a shadow of keen disappointment clouds her face. She turns abruptly, and once more gazes wistfully down the street.

The next thing Abbot sees is that the man is at her side; that he has accosted her; that she is startled and annoyed; and that although in totally different garb, her caller is no less a person than the secret-service official who visited him that morning. What on earth can that mean?

9

Whatever the conversation, it is very brief. Obedient to some suggestion or request, though not without one more quick glance at his window, Abbot sees her turn and enter the house. Quickly she passes the doorway and speeds along the hall. Regardless of the opinions and probable remarks of the gossipers in the sitting-room, Major Abbot hastens to the entrance and gazes after her until the graceful form is out of sight. Then he turns and confronts the sauntering detective—

" I did not know you knew Miss Warren," he says.

" I don't," is the answer. " Neither do you, do you ?"

" Well, we never met before yesterday, but—"

" You never wrote to her, did you, or to her father ?"

" Never, and yet I think there is a matter connected with it all that will require explanation."

" So do I. One of the worst points against the old gentleman is that very bad break he made in claiming that you had been a constant correspondent of his and of his daughter's."

" *One* of the worst ! Why, what is he accused of ?"

" Being a rebel spy—not to put too fine a point upon it."

Abbot stands aghast a moment.

" Why, man, it's simply impossible! I tell you, you're all wrong."

" Wish you'd tell my chief that," answers the man, impassively. " I don't like the thing a particle. They've got points up at the office that I know nothing about, and, probably, have more yet, now; for the package of papers was found upon him just as described from Frederick."

" What papers ?"

" Don't know. They've taken them up to the office. That's what makes the case rather weak in my eyes; no man would carry a packet of implicating papers in the pocket of his overcoat all this time. Such a package was handed to him as he left the tavern there by the landlord's wife, and she got it from the rebel spy who escaped back across the Potomac the next morning. He's the man your Colonel Putnam so nearly captured. Doctor Warren broke down on the back trip, it seems, and was delirious here for some days; but even then I should think he would hardly have kept these papers in an overcoat pocket, unless they were totally forgotten, and *that* would look vastly like innocence of their contents, which is what he claimed."

"Do you mean that he knows it? Has he been accused?" asks Abbot.

"Certainly. That's what I came down here for; he wanted his daughter. He is perfectly rational and on the mend now, and as the physicians said he would be able to travel in a day or two, it was decided best to nail him. There are scores of people hereabouts who'll stand watching better than this old doctor, to my thinking; but we are like you soldiers, and have our orders."

"Was my father up there when he was notified of his arrest," asks Abbot.

"No; Mr. Abbot has gone over to Senator Wilson's. He was met by a messenger while standing in the office a while ago."

The major tugs his mustache in nervous perplexity a moment. He needs to see the doctor. He cannot rest satisfied now until he has called upon him, assured him of his sympathy, his faith in his innocence, and his desire to be of service. More than that, he longs to tell him that he believes it in his power to explain the whole complication. More and more it is dawning upon him that he has had an arch-enemy at work in this missing Hollins, and that his villainy has involved them all.

"Can I see Dr. Warren?" he suddenly asks.

"I don't know. I am not directly in charge, but I will ask Hallett, who is up at the room now."

"Do; and come to my room and let me know as soon as you can."

In less than five minutes the officer is down at his door.

"I declare I wish you *would* come up. It seems more than ever to me that there's a blunder somewhere. The old man takes it mighty hard that he should be looked upon as a spy by the government he has suffered so much for. He says his only son was killed; captain in a New York regiment."

"Yes, and I believe it. I knew him at college."

"Well, if that don't beat all! And now that pretty girl is all he has left, and she's breaking her heart because she don't know how to comfort him."

"Come on," says Abbot. "I know the way."

And, for a lame man, he manages to make

marvellous time through the hallway and up that little flight of stairs. The room door is open as before. A man is pacing restlessly up and down the hall. There is a sound of sobbing from within, and, never stopping to knock, Paul Abbot throws off his cloak and enters.

She is bending over the bedside, mingling entreaty and soothing words with her tears; striving to induce her raging old father to lay himself down and take the medicine that the panic-stricken nurse is vainly offering. The doctor seems to have but one thought—wrath and indignation that he, the father of a son who died so gallantly, should have been accused of so vile a crime; he has but one desire, to rise and dress, and confront his accusers. If ever man needed the strong arm of a son to rest on at this moment, it is poor old Warren. If ever woman needed the aid and presence of a gallant lover, it is this sweet, half-distracted Bessie; and if ever man looked thoroughly fit to fill all requirements, it is the self-same young major of staff who comes striding in and grasping the situation with a soldier's glance.

Heaven! How her eyes light and beam at sight of him! How even through her tears, the flush of hope and joy springs to her cheek. How eagerly, trustfully, she turns to him, as though knowing all must now be well.

"Oh, papa! here is Mr. Abbot," she exclaims, and says it as though she felt that nothing more could ever be needed.

He steps between her and the staring eyes of the old gentleman; bends quickly down over him.

"Yes, doctor. Paul Abbot, whom you thought killed," and he gives him a significant glance; a glance that warns him to say no word that might undeceive her. "I have just had news of this extraordinary charge. I've come to you, quick as legs can carry me, to tell you that you are to lie perfectly still, and rest this burden with me. Don't stir; don't worry; don't say one word. I'm going straight to the provost-marshal's to tell them what I know, and explain away this whole thing. A most extraordinary piece of scoundrelism is at the bottom of it all, but I am beginning to understand it, fully. Doctor, will you trust me? Will you let me try and be Guthrie to you to-night; and promise me to lie still here until I come back from the provost-marshal's?"

"Do, father!" implores Bessie, bending over him, too.

There is a look of utter bewilderment in the doctor's haggard face, but he says no word. For a moment he gazes from one to the other, then drops back upon the pillow, his eyes fixed on Abbot's face.

"I am all unstrung, weak as a child," he murmurs; "I cannot understand; but do as you will."

There are voices in the hall; the clink of spurs and sabre; and a cavalry orderly makes his appearance at the door.

"I was to give this to Major Abbot, instantly," he says, saluting and holding forth an envelope. Abbot takes and tears it open. The message is brief enough, but full of meaning:

"Your presence necessary here at once to explain the papers found on Doctor Warren. Looks like a case of mistaken identity."

It is signed by the young officer whom he met on the occasion of his last visit.

"I thought so, doctor!" he says, triumphantly. "They are shaky already, and send for me to come. Depend upon it I'll bring you glad tidings in less than no time, and have an end to these mysteries. Now try and rest."

" A cavalry orderly makes his appearance at the door "

Then he turns to her. Can he ever forget the trust, the radiance, the restfulness in the shy, sudden look she gives him? His heart bounds with the sight; his pulse throbs hard as he holds forth his hand, and, for the first time, her soft warm palm is clasped in his.

"Don't worry one bit, Miss Bessie; we'll have this matter straightened out at once."

Then there is a pressure he cannot resist; a shy, momentary answer he cannot mistake; and, with his veins all thrilling, Paul Abbot goes forth upon his mission, leaving her looking after him with eyes that plainly say, "There walks a demi-god."

At the office he is promptly ushered into the presence of three or four men, two of them in uniform.

"Major Abbot, here is a packet of letters in a lady's hand, addressed to you. They were found on Doctor Warren, in the very pocket where he placed the package that was given him at Frederick. Have you lost such, or can you account for them?"

"I can account for them readily," answers Abbot, promptly. "They are mine, written by Miss Warren, and were stolen from me, as I believe; was there no explanation or address?"

"Nothing but this," is the answer, and the speaker holds forth a wrapper inside which is written these words:

"For your daughter. Ruined though I am, I can never forgive myself for the fearful wrong I have done her. Tell her it was all a lie. He never wrote, and she will never know the man who did."

Abbot stands staring at the paper, his hands clinching, his mouth setting hard. No word is spoken for a moment. Then, in answer to a courteous question, he looks up.

"It is as I thought. His villainy has involved others besides me. Doctor Warren is no more spy than I am. This writing is that d——d scoundrel Hollins's, who deserted from our regiment."

IX.

It is late that evening when Major Abbot returns to Willard's. He has found time to write a brief note to the doctor, which it was his intention to send by the orderly who bears the official order releasing the Warrens from surveillance. It suddenly occurs to him, however, that she may see the note. If so, what will be her sensations on finding that the handwriting is utterly unlike that in which all her letters had come to her. Abbot tears it into shreds, and contents himself with a message, saying that he is compelled to see the adjutant-general on immediate business, but will soon be with them.

It is true that the adjutant-general has business with Major Abbot, but it is some time before audience is obtained. There is still a whirl of excitement over Stuart's movements, and it is ten o'clock before the young officer is able to see his chief. The general is courteous, but a trifle formal and cold. Staff officers, he says, are now

G

urgently needed, and he desires to know how soon the major will feel able to resume duty.

"At once, sir," is the answer.

"But you are still far from strong, and— I do not mean office duty here; we have abundance of material for that sort of work."

"Neither do I, sir. I mean duty at the front. I can sit around headquarters in the field as comfortably as I can anywhere, and, to the best of my observation, the duty performed by the adjutant-general at corps or division headquarters is not such as involves much physical exertion."

The general smiles benignantly upon the younger officer, and with the air of a man who would say, "How little you know of the importance and responsibilities of the labors to which we are assigned; but you will soon understand."

"But can you ride yet?" he asks.

"I can; if a forward movement is in contemplation; and every day will bring me strength," answers Abbot. "In brief, general, if you have a post for me at the front I can go at once."

"One other thing. Have you any idea of the whereabouts of Mr. Hollins of your old regiment, or can you give us any idea as to where he would be likely to go? He has forwarded his resignation, dated Keedysville, Maryland, September 18. It was post-marked Baltimore, October 8, and came direct. Of course it cannot be accepted. What is needed is some clew as to his movements. Could he or would he have gone back to Boston? Had he anything to draw him thither?"

Abbot reflects a moment. "I can form no idea where he has gone," he answers.

"It was proposed to send an officer of your regiment back to confer with the police authorities, Major Abbot, and there are reasons why I prefer you should go. A few days' visit at your old home may not be unacceptable, and you can probably render valuable service. I have been told that there is reason to believe that Lieutenant Hollins is lurking somewhere around Boston at this very minute, and that is the first duty on which you are needed. Your instructions can be written later. Now can you go in the morning?"

There is a moment's silence. This is not the duty which Major Abbot expected, nor is it at all what he desires. He wonders if his father has not been in collusion with the senator, and, between the two, if some pretext has not been devised to get him home for a few days. It looks vastly that way.

"I confess that my hopes were in the opposite direction, general. I had visions of immediate employment at the front, when you spoke."

The bureau official is evidently pleased. He likes the timber the younger soldier is made of, and his grim, care-worn face relaxes.

"Major Abbot, you shall have your wish, and, depend upon me, the moment there is prospect of a forward move you shall join a division at the front. Your old colonel will have one this very week if it can be managed here, and he will be glad of your services; but I tell you, between ourselves, that I do not believe McClellan can be made to budge an inch from where he stands until positive orders are given from here. You go —not on leave, but on duty—for a week, and then we'll have work for you in the field. I have promised it."

Then the bewildered young major is notified that his father is waiting for him at the senator's, and thither he drives, half determined to upbraid them both; but the delight in the old gentleman's face is too much for him. It is nearly eleven when they reach Willard's, and, before he will consent to pack his soldier kit, Paul Abbot goes at once to the Warrens' room, and his father follows.

The secret-service man has gone. The physician is there and the nurse, both conversing with their patient, when the two gentlemen appear. Major Abbot presents his father and looks around the room somewhat disappointedly. Despite his excitement of the day, and possibly because of it, Doctor Warren seems in higher spirits and better condition than Abbot has imagined it possible for him to be. The two old gentlemen shake hands, and Mr. Abbot speedily seats himself by the side of the invalid, and frees himself of his impressions as to the extraordinary charges that had been preferred, and his satisfaction at their speedy refutation. The local physician, in low tones, is assuring Major Abbot that a day or two will restore their patient to strength sufficient to journey homewards, and that he believes the "set back" of the early evening will be of no avail if he can get him to sleep by midnight. Abbot hastily explains that he leaves at daybreak for Boston, and had only come in fulfilment of a promise. Then he accosts his father.

"I know we have both a great deal to say to Doctor Warren, father, but it is a pleasure only to be deferred. We must say good-night, so that he can sleep, and will meet in New York next week."

Doctor Warren looks up inquiringly. He is far from willing to let them go, but the physician interposes. They say their adieux and still Abbot hesitates; his eyes wander to the door which communicates with Bessie's room, and, as though in answer, it opens and she softly enters.

"I am so glad you have come," he says, in low, eager tone. "Let me present my father," and the old gentleman bows with courtly grace and comes forward to take her hand. She is a lovely picture to look at, with the sweet, shy consciousness in her face. The very gaze in Abbot's eyes has sent the color to her brows, and he holds her hand until he has to transfer it to his father's outstretched palm.

"The doctor tells us we must not stay, Miss Bessie," he continues, "but I could not go without a word. I am ordered to Boston by first train in the morning, but shall see you—may I not—in New York?"

Brave as she is, it comes too suddenly—this

news that she must part with her knight just as he has done her such loyal service, and before she has even thanked him by look or word. All the radiance, all the bright color fades in an instant, and Paul Abbot cannot but see it and divine, in part at least, the reason. He has in his pocket letters from her own fair hand, that he knows were written for him, and yet that he has no right to see. He reads in her lovely eyes a trust in him, a pain at this sudden parting, that he thrills in realizing, yet should steel his heart against or be no loyal man. But he cannot go without a word from her, and it is a moment before she can speak :

"Is—is it not very sudden? I shall never thank you enough for what you have done for father—for *us*, this evening. What would we have done without you?"

"That is nothing. There is no time now—but next week—New York—I may see you there, may I not?"

May he not? What man can look in her eyes and ask less? He holds her hand in close pressure one instant and hastens from the room.

Forty-eight hours later he is in the presence

10

of the woman who had promised to be his wife. The evening has seemed somewhat long. She was out when he called at an earlier hour, but was to be found at a dinner-party in the neighborhood. Major Abbot feels indisposed to meet her in presence of "society," and leaves word that he will return at ten o'clock. He finds her still absent and has to wait. Mr. Winthrop is at his club; Mrs. Winthrop has begged to be excused— - she had retired early with a severe headache. She does not want to see me, thinks Abbot, and that looks as though Viva were obdurate. It is a matter that has served to lose its potency for ill, and the major is angered at himself because of a thrill of hope; because of the thought of another face that *will* intrude. It is nearly eleven o'clock when he hears the rumble of carriage wheels at the door. He steps to the front window and looks out upon the pavement. Yes, there is the old family carriage drawn up in front in the full glare of the gas lamp. The footman is opening its door and Viva Winthrop steps quickly forth, glances up and down the street as though expectant of some one's coming, and turns quickly to speak to some one in the carriage. Abbot recognizes the face at the open window as that of an old family friend nodding good-night. The footman still stands, but Viva speaks to him; he touches his hat respectfully, but in some surprise, and then springs to his perch; the two ladies nod and exchange cordial good-nights again, and away goes the carriage, leaving Miss Winthrop standing on the sidewalk, where she is still searchingly looking up and down and across the street. As though in answer there comes springing through the dim light the hulking, slouching, round-shouldered figure of a big man. He is across the street and at her side in a few vigorous leaps, and away as quick as he came. No word has been interchanged, no sign on his part. He has handed her a small white parcel. She has placed in his hand a dark roll of something that he eagerly seizes and makes off with. It all happens before Abbot has time to realize what is going on, then she scurries up the stone steps and rings the bell. His first impulse is to go and open the door himself, but that will produce confusion. She will have no time to dispose of that packet, and Major Abbot will not take advantage of what he has inadvertently seen. He hears the old butler shuffling along the marble hallway, and his deferential announcement.

G*

"Mr. Abbot is in the parlor, Miss Winthrop."

And then he steps forward under the chande-lier to meet her.

It is a moment before she enters. Evidently his coming is a shock for which she is unprepared. She comes in with swiftly changing color and lips that tremble despite the unflinching courage of her eyes.

"This is indeed a surprise," she says, as she gives him her hand. "Why — when did you come, and how did you come, and how well you look for a man who has had so much suffering— I mean from your wounds," she finishes, hurried-ly. It is all said nervously and with evident purpose of simply talking to gain time and think. "Won't you sit down? You must be so fatigued. Take this chair, it's so much more com-fortable than that one you are getting. Have you seen mamma! No? Why? Does she know you are here? Oh, true; she did speak of a headache before I went out. Mrs. Laight and I have been to dinner at the Farnham's and have just returned. Why didn't you come round there —they'd have been so delighted to see you? You know you are quite a hero now."

He lets her run on, sitting in silence himself,

and watching her. She continues her rapid, nervous talk a moment more, her color coming and going all the time, and then she stops as suddenly. "Of course you can answer no questions when I keep chattering like a magpie."

She is seated now on the sofa facing him, as he leans back in one of those old-fashioned easy-chairs that used to find their way into some parlors in the *ante-bellum* days. When silence is fully established, and she is apparently ready to listen, he speaks:

"I came to-night, Viva, and to see *you*. Did you get my letter?"

"Your last one, from Washington? Yes. It came yesterday."

"I have come to see the letters."

"What letters?"

"Those which you must have received or been shown in order to make you believe me disloyal to you."

"I have no such letters."

"Did you send them to me, Viva."

"No."

"What did you do with them?"

She hesitates, and colors painfully; then seeks to parry.

"How do you know I ever saw any letters?"

"Because nothing less could explain your action; nor does this justify it. Still, I am not here to blame you. I want to get at the truth. What did you do with them?"

"They—went back."

"When? Before or after you got my letter?"

No answer for a moment, then:

"Why do you ask that? What possible difference can it make? They were shown me in strict confidence. I had long believed you cared more for another girl than you did for me, and these letters proved it."

"I do not admit that, Viva," is the grave, almost stern reply. "But do you mean that, after receiving my letter, you returned those that I asked for—that I had a right to see?"

"They were called for; and they were not mine to do as I chose with."

"Will you tell me how and by whom they were called for?"

He has risen now, and is standing under the chandelier, drawn to his full height.

"I do not wish to speak of it further. I have told the person that you denied the truth of them, and that is enough."

"I am sorry that you mentioned me to the person, or weighed my statements in any such scale."

"Paul Abbot!" she breaks in impetuously, rising too. "You say you never wrote to this girl, and I believe you; but tell me this: have you never seen her? do you not at this moment care for her infinitely more than you do for me?"

He considers a moment. It is a leading question; one he had not expected; but he will not stoop to the faintest equivocation. Still, he wants her to understand.

"Listen, Viva. Up to the time of your letter's coming she was a stranger to me. Now I have met her. She and her father were in the same hotel with us at Washington; and she, too, has been victimized by forged letters as you have."

"Enough, enough! Why not end it where it is? You know well that if you cared for me *that* would be the first assurance. Granted that we have both been cheated, fooled, tricked, why keep up the farce of a loveless engagement? That, at least, must end *now*."

"Even if it should, Viva, I am not absolved from a duty I owe you. It is my conviction that you have been drawn into a correspondence with a man against whom it is my solemn right and duty to warn you at once. You have no brother. For Heaven's sake be guided by what I say. Whatever may have been his influence in the past, you can never in the future recognize Mr. Hollins. If not captured by this time, he is a disgraced exile and deserter."

"He is nothing of the kind! You, and imperious men like you, denied to him the companionship of his brother officers, and his sensitive nature could not stand it. He has resigned and left the service, that is all."

"You are utterly mistaken, Viva. What I tell you is the solemn truth. For your name's sake I implore you tell me what has been his influence in the past. I well know he can be nothing to you in the future, Viva. You are not in communication with him now, are you?"

A ring at the bell. The old butler comes sleepily shuffling along the hall again, and appears at the parlor with a telegram. "They sent it after you, sir," is the explanation. Abbot, with curious foreboding, opens, and hurriedly reads the words,

"Rix also deserted; is believed to have gone to Boston."

"Viva!" he exclaims, "the man you gave that packet to was Rix, another deserter. My God! Do you *know* where Hollins is?"

But Viva Winthrop has fallen back on the sofa, covering her face with her hands.

X.

MAJOR ABBOT's stay in Boston is but brief. He had a hurried conference with the police late at night, after his painful interview with Miss Winthrop, and there is lively effort on part of those officials to run down the bulky stranger to whom she had intrusted that packet. There has been a family conference, too, between the elders of the households of Abbot and Winthrop, and the engagement is at an end. Coming in suddenly from his club, Mr. Winthrop entered the parlor immediately after the receipt of the telegram, and he is overwhelmed with consternation at the condition of affairs. He has insisted on a full statement from Viva's lips, and to her mother the story has been told. She withholds no point that is at all material, for her pride has been humbled to the dust in the revelation that has come to her. She is not the first woman, nor is she at all liable to be the last, to undertake the task of championing a man against the verdict of his

associates, and the story is simple enough. With
his sad, subdued manner, his air of patient suffering, and his unobtrusive but unerring attentions, Mr. Hollins had succeeded in making a
deep impression while they were abroad. Not
that her heart was involved; she protests against
that; but her sympathy, her pity, was aroused.
He had never inflicted his confidences upon her,
but had deftly managed to rouse her curiosity,
and make her question. By the time they returned to America she believed him to be a sensitive gentleman, poor, talented, struggling, and
yet burdened with the support of helpless rela-
tives, too distant of kin for her father's notice.
She had come back all aflame with patriotic fer-
vor, too; and his glowing words and soldierly
longings had inspired her with the belief that here
was a man who only needed a start and fair treat-
ment to enable him to rise to distinction in his
country's service. Through her father's influence he was commissioned in the —th, then
being organized, and in her friendship she had
sought to make his path easy for him. But he
was certainly deep in her confidence even then,
and shrewd enough to take advantage of it. He
had frequently written before, and it was not un-

natural he should write after the regiment left for the front—letters which intimated that he was far from content among his associates, which hinted at distress of mind because he daily saw and heard of things which would cause bitter sorrow to those who had the right to command his most faithful services. He had shown deep emotion when informed of her engagement to Mr. Abbot, and it was hard to confess this. It soon became apparent to her that he desired her to understand that he deeply loved her, and was deterred only by his poverty from seeking her hand. Then came letters that were constructed with a skill that would have excited the envy of an Iago, hinting at other correspondences on part of Mr. Abbot and of neglects and infidelities that made her proud heart sore. Still there were no direct accusations; but, taken in connection with the long periods of apparent silence on his part and the unloverlike tone of his letters when they reached her, the hints went far to convince her that she had promised her hand to a careless and indifferent wooer. This palliated in her mind the disloyalty of which she was guilty towards him, and at last, in the summer just gone, she had actually written to Mr. Hol-

lins for proofs of his assertions. For a long time
—for weeks—he seemed to hold back, but at last
there came three letters, written in a pretty, girl-
ish hand. She shrank from opening them, but
Mr. Hollins, in his accompanying lines, simply
bade her have no such compunction. They had
been read by half a dozen men in camp already,
and the girl was some village belle who possibly
knew no better. She did read, just ten lines, of
one of them, and was shamed at her act as she
was incensed at her false *fiancé*. The ten lines
were sweet, pure, maidenly words of trust and
gratitude for his praise of her heroic brother;
and in them and through them it was easy for
the woman nature to read the budding love of a
warm-hearted and innocent girl.

This roused her wrath, and would have led to
denunciation of him but for the news of his
wounds and danger. Then came other letters
from Hollins, hinting at troubles in which he
was involved; and then, right after Antietam,
he seemed to cease to write for a fortnight, and
his next letter spoke of total change in all his
prospects—resignation from the service, serious
illness, possibly permanently impaired health,
and then of suffering and want. A foul accusa-

tion had been trumped up against him by enemies in the regiment; he was alleged to have
stolen letters belonging to officers. In part it
was true. He had bribed a servant to get those
three letters which he sent her, that she might
be saved from the fate that he dreaded for her.
It was for her sake he had sinned; and now he
implored her to keep his secret, and to return to
him all his letters on that subject, as well as those
he had sent as proofs. He dare not trust them
to the mails, but a faithful friend, though a poor
man like himself, would come with a note from
him, and he would be a trusty bearer. The friend
had come but the morning of Abbot's arrival.
He humbly rang at the basement door; sent up
a note; and, recognizing Hollins's writing, she
had gone down and questioned him. He sadly
told her that the quartermaster was in great
trouble. "His enemies had conspired against
him;" his money accounts were involved, and
there lay the great difficulty. Mr. Hollins
would never forgive him, said the man, if he
knew he was hinting at such a thing, but what
he needed to help him out of his trouble was
money. It made her suspicious, but she reread
the note. "He is devoted to me, and perfectly

reliable. I have cared for him and his sister from childhood. Do not fear to trust the letters, or anything you may write, to him."

Mr. Hollins was too proud ever to ask for money and could not contemplate the possibility of its being asked in his behalf, she argued. But if anything she might write was to be trusted to the messenger, surely she could trust his statements, and so she questioned eagerly. The bearer thought a thousand dollars might be enough to straighten everything, and she bade him be at the front of the house that night by half after ten, to bring her a little packet he spoke of as having received from Hollins—her own letters to him—and the money would be ready. There was something about the man's face and carriage that was familiar. She could not tell where she had seen him, but felt sure that she had, and it seemed to her that it was in uniform. But he denied having ever been in service, and seemed to shrink into shadow as though alarmed at the idea. During the day she got the money from the bank and gave it, as Abbot saw, and then when the telegram came it all flashed across her —the messenger was indeed Rix. Rix was a deserter beyond all peradventure. Then, doubtless, she was all wrong and Abbot all right as to the real status of Mr. Hollins. No wonder she was overwhelmed.

But in all her self-abasement and distress of mind Viva Winthrop was clear-headed on the question of the dissolution of that engagement. "He does not love me and I do not deserve that he should," was her epitome of the situation. "It will cause him no sorrow now, and it must be ended." And it was. He called and asked to see her, if she felt well enough to receive him; he acquiesced in her decision, but he wanted to part as friends. She begged to be excused, explaining that she had not left her rooms since the night of his arrival, which was true. And now, with a heart that beats more joyously despite the major's proper and conscientious effort to believe that he is not happier in his freedom, he is hastening back to the front, for his orders have come.

Two things remain to be attended to before reporting for duty. He makes every effort to find Hollins's hiding-place, but without avail. Miss Winthrop tells him that beyond the post-mark, Baltimore, there is not a clew in any of the letters, and that they have ceased coming entire-

ly. Rix made no mention beyond saying that
he was in Baltimore among people who would
guard him, and Rix himself has gone—no man
can say whither.

The other matter is one to which he hastens
with eager heart. Twice he has written to Doctor Warren since their parting at Washington,
and he has asked permission to call upon them at
Hastings before returning. His orders come before any reply. He therefore writes to Hastings
the day before he leaves home, begging that a
telegram be sent to meet him at the Metropoli-
tan, the war-time rendezvous of army men when
in New York on leave, and his face is blank with
disappointment when the clerk tells him that no
telegram has been received. He has a day at
his disposal, and he loses no time, but goes up
the river by an afternoon train, and returns by
the evening "accommodation" with uneasy heart.
Doctor Warren and Miss Bessie had not yet come
back was the news that met him at the pretty
little homestead. The doctor had been ill in
Washington, and when he was well enough to
start the young lady was suddenly taken down.
Abbot is vaguely worried. He anxiously questions the kindly old housekeeper, and draws from
11

her all that she knows. She is looking for letters any moment; but the last one was from Willard's, four days since, saying they would have to stay. Miss Bessie was suddenly taken ill. Won't the gentleman come in? and she will get the letter. He takes off his cloak and forage cap, and steps reverently into the little sitting-room, wherein every object is bathed in the sunshine of late afternoon, and everywhere he sees traces of her handiwork. There on the wall is Guthrie's picture; there hangs his honored sword and the sash he wore when he led the charge at Seven Pines. With the soldier-spirit in his heart, with the thrill of sympathy and comradeship that makes all brave men kin, Abbot stands before that silent presentment of the man he knew at college, and slowly stretches forth his hand and reverently touches the sword-hilt of the buried officer. He is not unworthy; he, too, has led in daring charge, and borne his country's flag through a hell of carnage. They are brothers in arms, though one be gathered already into the innumerable host beyond the grave. They are comrades in spirit, though since college days no word has ever passed between them, and Abbot's eyes fill with emotion he cannot repress as he thinks how bitter a loss this son and brother has been to the stricken old father and fragile sister. Ah! could he but have known, that day on the Monocacy; could he but have read the truth in the old man's eyes, and accepted as a fact his share of that mysterious correspondence rather than have unwillingly dealt so cruel a blow! His lips move in a short, silent prayer, that seems to well up from his very heart; and then the housekeeper is at his side, and here is the doctor's letter. It is too meagre of detail for his anxiety. He reads it twice, but it is all too brief and bare. He is recalled to himself again. The housekeeper begs pardon, but she is sure this must be Mr. Abbot, whose letters were so eagerly watched for all the time before they went away. She had heard in the village he was killed, and she is all a-quiver now, as he can see, with excitement and suppressed feeling at his resurrection. Yes, this is Mr. Abbot, he tells her, and he is going straight to Washington that he may find them. And she shows him pictures of Bessie in her girlhood, Bessie at school, Bessie in the bonnie dress she wore at the Soldiers' Fair. Yes, he remembers having seen that very group before, at Edwards's Ferry, before Ball's Bluff. She prattles about Bessie, and of

11

Bessie's going for his letters, and how she cried over them. He is all sympathy, and bids her say on as he moves about the room, touching little odds-and-ends that he knows must be hers; and he is loath to go, but eager too, since it is to carry him back to her. He writes a few lines on a card to tell them of his visit and his orders, should they fail to meet; he begs the doctor to write, and warns him that he must expect frequent letters; and then, with one long look about the sunlit, love-haunted room, with one appeal for brotherly sympathy in his parting gaze at Guthrie Warren's picture, he strides back to the station, and by sunrise of another day is hurrying to Washington. In his breast-pocket he carries the compact little wad of letters, all addressed to himself, all written in her own delicate and dainty hand, yet sealed from his eyes as securely as though locked in casket of steel. Though he longs inexpressibly to read their pages and to better know the gentle soul that has so suddenly come into his life, they are not his to open. What would he not give for one moment face to face with the man who had lured and tricked her—and with his name!

They are not at Willard's, says the clerk, when

Major Abbot arrives and makes his inquiries. The doctor paid his bill that morning and they were driven away, but he does not think they left town. Yes, telegrams and letters both had come for the doctor, and the young lady had been confined to her room a few days, and was hardly well enough to be journeying now. Abbot's orders require him to report at the War Department on the following day, and he cannot go to rest until he has found their hiding-place. Something tells him that she has at last discovered the fraud of which she has been made the victim, and he longs to find her—longs to tell her that if the real Paul Abbot can only be accepted in lieu of the imaginary there need be no break in that strange correspondence; he is ready to endorse anything his fraudulent double may have written provided it be only love and loyalty to her.

It is late at night before he has succeeded in finding the hack driver who took them away, and by him is driven to the house wherein they have sought refuge. All distressed as he is at thought of their fleeing from him, Paul Abbot finds it sweet to sit in the carriage which less than twelve hours ago bore her over these self-same dusty streets. He bids the hackman rein up when he gets to the corner, and wait for him. Then he pushes forward to reconnoitre. Lights are burning in many rooms, but the neighborhood is very silent. Far down an intersecting avenue the band of some regiment is serenading a distinguished senator or representative from the state from which they hail, and Abbot can hear the cheers with which the great man is greeted as he comes forth to tender his acknowledgments, and invite the officers and such of his fellow-citizens as may honor him, to step in and "have something." It is a windy night in late October. The leaves are whirling in dusty spirals and shutters bang with unmelodious emphasis, and all the world seems dreary; yet, to him, with love lighting the way, with the knowledge that the girl he has learned to worship is here within these dull brick walls, there is a thrill and vigor in every nerve. No light burns in the hallway; none in the lower floor of the number to which he has been directed. He well knows it is too late to call, even to inquire for them, but the army has moved, and at last is pushing southward again, feeling its way along the Blue Ridge, and he so well knows that the morrow must send him forward to resume his duties. If he cannot see *her*, it will be comfort, at least, to see her father. He is half disposed to ring and ask for him when a figure comes around a neighboring corner and bears slowly down upon him. The night lamps are dull and flickering and the stranger is a mere shadow. Where Major Abbot stands enveloped in the cloak-cape of his army overcoat there is no light at all. Whoever may be the approaching party he has the disadvantage of being partially visible to a watcher whose presence he cannot be aware of until close at hand. When he has come some yards farther Abbot is in no doubt as to his identity, and steps forward to greet him.

"Doctor Warren, I am so glad to have found you, for I must hurry after the army to-morrow, and only reached Washington this evening. Tell me, how is Miss Bessie?"

The doctor is startled, as a matter of course, but there is something in the young soldier's directness that pleases him. Perhaps he is pleased, too, to know that his own views are correct, and that the moment Paul Abbot reached Washington he has come in search of them. He takes the proffered hand and holds it—or, rather, finds his firmly held.

"Bessie has been ill, but is better, major; and how did you leave them all at home? I have just been taking a walk of two or three blocks before turning in. Fresh air is something I cannot do without. How did you find us?"

"By hunting up your hackman. I was grievously disappointed at not finding you at Hastings, where I went first, or here at Willard's. Did you not get my letters and telegrams?"

"They were forwarded, and came last night."

"Then you moved this morning to avoid me, doctor. Does it mean that I am to be punished for another man's crime? Guthrie's picture had no such unfriendly welcome for me, and I do not believe you want to hide her from me. Tell me what it is that makes Bessie avoid me of her own accord. Has she heard the truth about the old letters?"

Doctor Warren is silent a moment, looking up into the young soldier's face. Then he more firmly grasps his hand.

"I do *not want* to avoid you, Abbot, but it is only natural that now she should find it hard to meet you. Three days after you left she caught me fairly, and finding that the letter in my hand was yours, she noted instantly the difference between the writing and that of the letters that came to her at home. Something else had roused her suspicions, and I had to tell her that there had been trickery, and she would have no half-way explanation. She probed and questioned with a wit as keen as any lawyer's. She made me confess that that was why I told her Paul Abbot was dead when I got back to her at Frederick. He was dead to us. And so, little by little, it all came out, and she was simply stunned for a while. It made her too ill to admit of our travelling, and she made me tell her when you were expected back, and bring her here. In a day or two we will start homeward."

"And meantime I shall have had to start for the front. Doctor Warren, give her this little package—her own letters. Tell her that I have read no line of one of these, but that, until I can win for myself letters in her dear hand there will be no peace or happiness for me. These are the letters that were sent to you at Frederick, with a few remorseful lines, from the scoundrel who wrought all the trouble. His original motive was simply to injure me, in the hope that he might profit by it. He sought to break an engagement of marriage that existed between me and Miss Winthrop, of Boston. Before he succeeded in making this breach it is my belief that he had become so touched and charmed by the letters she wrote that even his craven heart was turned to see its own baseness. He had every opportunity of tampering with our mail. He felt, when I was left wounded at the Monocacy, that that would end the play; and then, in his despair and remorse, he deserted. He was around Frederick a day or two in disguise, and sought to see you and her. Failing in that, he sent you by the landlady the packet that was afterwards taken from your overcoat by the secret-service men; and the next thing he came within an ace of being captured by his own colonel. Escaping, he was believed to be a rebel spy, and so implicated you. It was to search for him I was sent to Boston. There Miss Winthrop formally broke our engagement, and I would be a free man to-day, doctor, but for your daughter; and now it is not freedom I seek, but a tie that only death can break. You came to Paul Abbot when you thought him sorely wounded, and she came with you. Now that he is sore stricken he comes to you. If it will pain her I will ask no meeting now, but don't you think I owe her a good many letters, doctor? Won't you let me pay that debt?"

It is a long speech for Abbot, but his heart is full. The old gentleman's sad face seems to thaw and beam under the influence of his frank avowal and that winning plea. Abbot has held forth his other hand, and there the two men stand, both trembling a little, under the influence of a deep and holy emotion, clasping each other's hands and looking into each other's face. They are at the very door-step of the old-fashioned boarding-house which was so characteristic a feature of the capital in the war-days. The door itself is but a few arms'-lengths away, and all of a sudden it softly opens, and, with a light mantle thrown over her shoulders, a tall, slender, graceful girl comes forth upon the narrow porch.

"Is that you, papa? I heard your step, and wondered why you remained outside. Was the door locked?"

There is an instant of silence. Then a young soldier, in his staff uniform, takes three quick, springing steps, and is at her side. The doctor seems bent on further search for fresh air, for he turns away with a murmured word to his trem-

II*

bling companion, and Bessie Warren finds it impossible to retreat. Major Abbot has seized her hand, and is saying—she hardly hears, she hardly knows, what. But it is all so sudden; it is all so sweet.

*" Then a young soldier in his staff uniform takes three
springing steps, and is at her side."*

XI.

COLD and gray in the mist of the morning the long columns have filed down from the heights, and are massed at the water's edge. It is chill December, and the frost has eaten deep into the ruddy soil of Virginia, but the Rappahannock flows swiftly along, uncrusted by the ice that fetters Northern streams, yet steaming in the biting air. Fog-wreaths rise from the rippling surface, and all along the crowded shore the clouds hang dense and heavy. Nowhere can one see in any direction more than a dozen yards away; all beyond is wrapped in swirling, eddying fog-bank. Here in the thronging ranks, close at hand, men speak in low tones as they stamp upon the frozen ground or whip their mittened hands across the broad blue chests to restore circulation and drive the ache and numbness away. Here and there are some who have turned their light blue capes up over their heads, and take no part in the low-toned chat. Leaning on their muskets, they let their thoughts go wandering far away, for all men know that bloody work is coming. The engineers are hammering at their bulky pontoons now, and down at the water's edge the clumsy boats are moored, waiting for chess and balk carriers to be told off, and the crews to man the heavy sweeps. Up on the heights to the rear, planted thickly on every knoll and ridge, are the black-mouthed guns, and around them are grouped the squads of ghostly, grisly, fog-dripping cannoneers. One may walk along that line of heights for mile after mile, and find there only grim ranges of batteries and waiting groups of men. All is silence; all is alertness; all is fog. Back of the lines of un-limbered cannon, sheltered as far as possible from returning fire, the drivers and horses and the heavy-laden caissons are shrouded in the mist-veil, and the staff officers, groping to and fro, have to ask their way from battery to battery, or go yards beyond their real objective point. Little fires are burning here and there, and bat-tery-lanterns are flickering in the gloom. Out on the face of the stream, too, one can see from the northern shore weird, dancing lights, like will-o'-the-wisps, go twinkling through the fog;

and far across the waters, from time to time,
there is heard the sudden crack of rifle. The
Southern pickets are beginning to catch faint
glimpses of those lights, and are opening fire, for
vigilant officers are there to interpret every sound
and sight, and with the first break of the wintry
dawn they grasp the meaning of the murmur
that has come for hours from the upper shore.
"The Yanks are laying bridges" is the word
that goes from mouth to mouth, and long before
the day is fairly opened the nearing sounds and
the will-o'-the-wisp lights out there in the fog
tell the shivering pickets that the foe is more
than half-way across. Daybreak brings strong
forces into line along the southern bank, all eyes
straining through the fog. Out to the front the
ping! ping! of the rifles has become rapid and
incessant, and by broad daylight all the river
bank and the walls of the buildings that command a view of it are packed with gray riflemen
ready for work the instant those bridge-heads
loom into view. When seven o'clock comes,
and the fog thins just a little, there are the bridge-
ends, sure enough, poking drearily into space, but
the only signs of the builders are the motionless
forms in blue that are stretched here and there

about the boats or planks, only faintly visible through the mist; the working parties have been forced to give it up. Back they come, what is left of them, and tell their tale among the sympathizing blue overcoats in the wearying ranks, and officers ride away up the slopes, and there are moments of suspense and question, and then the thud of sponge-staff and rammer among the batteries, and a sudden flash and roar, tearing the mists asunder; another, another; and then, up and down along the line of heights, the order goes, and gun after gun belches forth its charge of shot and shell, and back from the walls of Fredericksburg comes the direful echo and the crash of falling roof or gable. "Depress those muzzles!" is the growling order. "The whole bank is alive with rebs, and we must shell 'em out before those bridges can be finished." The elevating screws are spun in their beds, the shell fuzes cut down to the very edge. Some guns are so near the river that they are rammed with grape and canister; and so, for an hour, the thundering cannonade goes on, and the infantry crouch below, and swear and shiver, and once in a while set up a cheer when occasion seems to warrant it. And then, covered by this furious fog-bombardment, the engineers again push forward their bridge-builders, and cram their pontoons, and launch them forth upon the stream. It is all useless. No sooner do they reach the bridge-end when down they go by the dozens before the hot fire of a thousand Southern rifles. So dense is the fog that the gunners cannot aim. Shot, shell, and canister go shrieking through roof and wall, and ripping up streets and crossings; but the plucky riflemen hug the shore in stern determination, and again the bridges are abandoned.

And so a cold and cheerless morning ebbs away; and at last, towards noon, there comes relief. The sun bursts through the clouds, and licks up the fog-bank. The mist-veil is withdrawn, and there stands Fredericksburg, with shattered roof and spire, backed by a long line of gun-bristling heights, and there are the unfinished bridges jutting helplessly out two thirds across the water. A number of the heavy pontoons are still moored close to shore, and while all along under the bank the regiments are ranging into battle order, two or three of them are tumbling into those clumsy arks, cramming them with armed men, and then pushing off into the stream. Failing in working across a narrow

12

causeway, the "Yanks" are taking to their boats
and sending over a flotilla. It is a daring, desperate feat, but it tells. Despite the fierce resistance, despite the heavy loss that befalls them,
animated by the cheers of their comrades, they
push ahead, answering the fire as well as they
can, and at last, one after another, the boats are
grounded on the southern shore, and, though sadly diminished in numbers, the men leap forth
and go swarming up the bank, driving the gray
pickets to cover. Others hurry across and rein-
force them; then more and more, until they are
strong enough to seize the nearest buildings and
hold the approaches, and then the working parties leap forward; the bridge is finished with a
will, and the comrades of their brigade come
tramping cheerily across. Three splendid regiments are they which made that daring venture,
mere companies in numbers as compared with
their early strength, and one of them is the —th
Massachusetts, now led by a captain. Colonel
Putnam stands at his side at this moment of triumph and partial rest. He commands the brigade that has done this brilliant work, and now
is receiving the thanks sent over from corps headquarters; and the mounted officer, the first one

across the bridge, who bears the general's congratulations, is his young chief-of-staff, Major
Abbot.

There has been fierce fighting through the
streets, stubborn resistance on part of the occupants of the town, and determined effort on part
of the thronging force of Union men who are
constantly gaining accessions as the brigades
come marching over. Just at sunset, with the
town fully in their possession, there is sudden
turmoil and excitement among the blue-coats
gathered around an old brick building near the
western edge. There is rushing to and fro;
then savage exclamations, shouts of " Kill him !"
" Hang him !" " Run him down to the creek and
duck him !" and the brigade commander, with
Major Abbot and one or two other mounted officers, has quite as much as he can do to rescue
from the hands of an infuriated horde of soldiers
a bruised, battered, slouching hulk of a man in a
dingy Confederate uniform. He implores their
protection, and it is only when they see the piteous, haggard, upturned face, and hear the wail
of his voice, that Putnam and Abbot recognize
the deserter, Rix. Abbot is off his horse and by
his side in an instant. Sternly ordering back the

men who had grappled and were dragging him, the major holds Rix by the coat-collar and gazes at him in silent amaze.

"In God's name, how came you here, and in this garb?" he finally asks.

Weak with sickness, suffering, and the horrible fright he has undergone, the bully of former days simply shudders and cringes now. He crouches at Abbot's feet, gazing fearfully around him at the circle of vengeful, powder-blackened faces.

"Don't let them touch me, Mr. Abbot! Oh, for God's sake help me. I'm 'most dead, anyhow. I can't talk now. We're 'most starved, too, and Mr. Hollins is dying."

"Hollins!" exclaims Abbot, almost losing his hold on the collar and dropping the limp creature to earth. "What do you mean? where?"

"In there; in the bedroom up-stairs. Oh, major, don't leave me here; these men will murder me!" he implores, clutching the skirts of Abbot's heavy overcoat; but Colonel Putnam signals "Go on," and, leaving his abject prisoner, Abbot hastens up the stairs of the old brick house, and there, in a low-ceilinged room, stretched upon the bed, with wild, wandering eyes and fevered lips, with features drawn and ghastly, lies the man who

has so bitterly sinned against him, and whom he
has so often longed to meet eye to eye—but not
this way.

And it is an awful look of recognition that
greets him, too. Shot through and through as
he is, tortured with thirst and suffering, praying
for help and longing for the sight of some friend-
ly face, it seems a retribution almost too cruel
that, in his extreme hour, the man sent by Heav-
en to minister to his needs should be the one he
has so foully wronged, the one of whom he lives
in dread. He covers his eyes with a gesture of
dismay, and turns fearfully to the wall. There
is a moment of silence, broken only by the rattle
of the window in its casing as it shudders to the
distant boom of the guns far down the line.
Then Abbot steps to the bedside and places his
gauntleted hand upon the shoulder of the strick-
en man.

"Hollins! How are you wounded? Have
you seen a surgeon?"

No answer for a moment, and the question is
gently repeated.

"Shot through the body—rifle-ball. There
was a surgeon here last night, but he's gone."

"Lie still then until I get one. I would bring

Doctor Thorn, but he has too much to do with—too much to do just now." He comes near saying "with our own men," but checks himself in time. He cannot "kick the man that is down" with such a speech as that, and it is not long before he reappears, and brings with him a surgeon from one of the arriving regiments. Colonel Putnam, too, comes up the stairs, but merely to take a look at the situation, and place a guard over both the wounded man and his strange, shivering companion, Rix. Some of the soldiers are sent for water, and others start a fire in the little stove in the adjoining room. The doctor makes his examination, and does what he can for his sinking patient, but when he comes out he tells Abbot that Hollins has not many hours to live, "and he wants to see you," he adds. "Did you know him?"

There is a strange scene in the cramped little room of the quaint old house that night. By the light of two or three commissary candles and the flickering glare from the fire one can see the features of the watchers and of the fast-dying man. Abbot sits by the bedside; Colonel Putnam is standing at the foot, and the adjutant of the —th Massachusetts has been reading aloud from his notes the statement he has taken down from the lips of the former quartermaster. One part of it needs verification from authority not now available. Mr. Hollins avers that he is not a deserter to the enemy as appearances would indicate, but a prisoner paroled by them.

The statement, so far as it bears upon his official connection with the regiment, is about as follows:

"I had personal reasons for going back to the Monocacy—reasons that could not be explained to the satisfaction of a commanding officer. I *had* to see Mr. Abbot to explain a wrong I had done him, and avert, if possible, the consequences. I left without permission, and rode back, but found all the roads picketed, and I was compelled to hide with a farmer near Boonsboro until Rix reached me. He had been my clerk, and was an expert penman. He fixed the necessary papers for me, and, with the aid of certain disguises I had, it was not so hard to get around. I meant to resign, but feared that, if offered through the regular channels, it would be refused, and I be brought to trial because of the condition of my accounts. Then I found that I was too late to undo the wrong I had done, and it was while

trying to make partial amends that I came so
near being captured by Colonel Putnam at Frederick. It made me desperate. That night I took
the first horse I could find, and rode down the
valley, believing all was lost, and that I must get
away from that part of the country. Money
found me a hiding-place when my papers would
no longer serve. Then money bribed a messenger to carry word of my condition to Rix, who
had been sent to the regiment at Harper's Ferry.
He got away and joined me, and made out some
more papers for me, and then started, by night
and alone, to get home, where he said he had
money. Mine was about gone by that time, and
here I lay in hiding until Stuart came sweeping
down the Monocacy on his way back to Virginia,
and I was glad to be captured and carried along.
I gave him my proper name and rank, and when
Rix came back the army had left that part of
the country, and he followed me into Virginia.
He said he would be shot, anyway, if captured;
and the next I heard of him—I being then a
prisoner in Richmond—was that he had enlisted
in a Virginia regiment, and was dying here in
Fredericksburg. He had been devoted to me,
and needed me. I gave my parole, and was

allowed to come here to nurse him. He was recovering and able to be about when the bombardment opened, and I was shot at the river bank, whither I had gone to bid him good-bye, and was carried here. The rest that I have to say is for Major Abbot alone to hear."

Putnam and the adjutant, after a few questions, withdraw; and at last, with even the soldier nurse excluded, the dying man is alone with the one officer of his regiment who had striven to befriend him, and whom he has so basely rewarded.

"There is no time for lamenting or empty talk of forgiveness and remorse. It is time you heard the truth, Abbot. I always envied you at college. I envied every man who had birth or wealth or position. I had some brains, but was poor, burdened with the care of a vagabond brother who was well-nigh a jail-bird, and whose only talent was penmanship. He would have been a forger then if it hadn't been for me. For me he afterwards became one. You know who I mean now—Rix. Mr. Winthrop gave me opportunities, and I worked. I had little money, though, but time and again I was called to his house, saw his daughter, and I was ambitious.

When she went abroad I followed; was as discreetly attentive as my wit could make me—and when I failed to make the impression I hoped, and we returned, I learned the reason—she was engaged to you. It made me determine that I would undermine it. You did not love her, nor she you. It was a family match, and not one that would make either of you happy. My life in the regiment was a hell, because they seemed to—seemed to know me for what I was. And you simply tolerated me. It made a devil of me, Abbot, and I vowed that proud girl should love me and turn from you if I had to hang for the means that brought it about. I was quartermaster at Edwards's Ferry, and Rix was the man who fetched and carried the mails. 'Twas easy enough to abstract her letters or yours from time to time, but the case needed something more than that. Neglect would not rouse her; jealousy might. One day there came the picture of those girls at Hastings (Abbot's hands begin to clinch; he has listened coldly up to this point), and I saw the group that was sent to them, and the pretty letter written by their secretary, Miss Warren. Then came her letter saying she was Guthrie Warren's sister. I knew him well at college,

and an idea occurred to me. I took your picture, wrote a note, and had Rix copy it, and sent
it in your name. When the answer came Rix
and I were on the lookout for it, and got it, and
wrote again and again. I had matter enough to
work on with my knowledge of Warren, and
then his death intensified the interest. I don't
care to look in your face now, Abbot, for I'm
not a fearless man ; nothing but a beaten, broken,
cowardly scoundrel ; but I began trying on that
sweet and innocent country girl the arts against
which your *fiancée*, my highbred kinswoman, had
been proof; I was bound to punish *her* pride.
But I found my pretty correspondent as shy, as
maidenly and reserved, with all her sister-love
and pride, as the other was superior. It was
game worth bringing down, by Heaven! and I
grew desperate. I was drinking then, and getting snarled up in my accounts, and you had
turned a cold shoulder on me ; and then came
the campaign and Rix's break and more difficul-
ties, and I was at my wit's end to keep the letters from you ; and just before Second Bull Run
came Miss Winthrop's letters challenging me to
prove that you did not care for her, and I sent
her three of Miss Warren's letters. But, worse

I

than that, I had been wooing another in your name; and, because she would not betray an undue interest, I became more engrossed; became more warmly interested; and soon it was not for the sake of showing your *fiancée* a love-letter from another woman, but to satisfy the cravings of my own heart. I began more and more to strive to win this dainty, innocent, pure-minded girl. Aye, sir, I was wooing over your name; but 'twas *I* who loved; yes, loved her, Abbot. *Now*, what think you of me and what I suffered?"

He pauses a moment, choked and quivering. He motions with his hand to the cup of stimulant the doctor has left him. Abbot coldly hands it to him, and finds that he must raise him from the pillow before he can swallow. He is stirred to his inmost soul with wrath and indignation against this ruthless traitor, even when the fates have laid him low. It is hard to touch him gently, but he steps to his side and does what he can, bidding him use no exertion and be calm as possible. A few painful, hurried breaths, and then Hollins goes on again.

"Though not once had she confessed her love, I felt I was gaining. She sent me her photograph. It is here, on my breast; I have carried it day and night." Abbot's muscles grew rigid again and his stern face sets with a sterner look. "But I was in constant worry about my affairs and the coming of those letters. Then when you were wounded and left behind at South Mountain I felt that the crisis had come. I *had* to get back there. Something told me she would hasten to you. They came, and I had the agony of seeing him—her father—returning from his visit to you; Rix told me of it afterwards. Then I strove madly to see her; to tell her the truth, though I knew she would only despise and spurn me. I scrawled a note confessing my crime, but sending no name; gave it to the woman to give to the doctor, and then tore myself away. I was the rebel spy the colonel nearly caught, and from that time I have been a fugitive; and now—a chance shot ends it all. Rix has been faithful to me, poor devil, and I came here to do what I could for him. *Voila tout!* Abbot, don't let them shoot him. He isn't worth it. Give me more of that brandy."

He lies back on the grimy pillow, breathing fast and painfully. Abbot stands in silence a moment. Then his voice, stern and constrained, is heard in question:

"Have you any messages, Hollins? Is there any way in which I can serve you?"

"It seems tough—but the only friend I have to close my eyes is the man I plotted against and nearly despoiled of his lady-love," mutters Hollins. Either he is wandering a little bit or the brandy is potent enough to blur his sense of the nearness of death. "I wanted to tell you the truth—not that I look for forgiveness. I know your race well enough. You'll see fair play, but love and hate are things you don't change in much. I've no right to ask anything of you, but—who *is* there? My God! I believe your wife that is to be was about the only friend I had in the world—except Rix. He brought me back the letters, and says she was so good to him. I hope he didn't ask her for money. He swears he didn't, but he's such a liar! We both are, for that matter. I'm glad, though, now, that my lies didn't hurt you. They didn't, did they, Abbot? You're still engaged?"

"I—am engaged."

"Oh, well; if I only hadn't brought that damnable sorrow to that poor child, and if I could only feel that they wouldn't shoot Rix, it wouldn't be so bad—my going now. What *will* they do with Rix?"

"He must stand trial for desertion, I fancy. The men nearly lynched him as it was."

"I know, and you saved him. Isn't it all strange?" Here for over a year we two have been plotting against you, and now, at the last, you're the only friend we have. Where is he?"

"Down below, under guard. You shall see him whenever you feel like it. Is there any one else you want to see, Hollins?"

"Any one—any one? Ah, God! Yes, with a longing that burns. It is *her* face. It is she—Bessie!" His hand steals feebly into his breast, and he drags slowly forth a little packet of oiled silk. This he hugs close to his fluttering heart, and his eyes seek those of the young soldier standing there so strong, so self - reliant and erect. His glance seems envious, even now, with the fast - approaching angel's death - seal dimming their light, and the clammy dew gathering on his brow.

"It was your picture I sent her, just as you seem to stand there now. It was I who won her, but she thinks I looked like you."

"Pardon me, Hollins," breaks in Abbot, with a voice that trembles despite every effort at self-control, and trembles, too, through the very coldness of the tone. "Colonel Putnam is not far off. There are others whom you might like to see; and shall I send Rix to you?"

"No—not now—no use. Promise me this, Abbot. No matter where or how I'm buried—never mind coffin, or the flag, or the volleys, or the prayers; I don't deserve— They won't help me. *You* see to it, will you, that this is buried on my heart? It's her picture, and some letters. Promise."

Abbot slowly bows his head.

"I promise, Hollins, if it will comfort you."

"If there were only some way—some way to tell her. I loved her so. She might forgive when she knew how I died. You may see her, Abbot. Stop! take these three letters; they're addressed to you, anyway. Take them to her, by and by, and tell her, will you? but let the picture go with me."

The clutching fingers of one hand clasp about the slim envelope that contains the little photograph; the fingers of the other hand are plucking nervously at the blanket that is thrown over the dying man. There is another moment of silence, and then Abbot again asks him if he will have his brother brought to him. Hollins nods, and Abbot goes to the door and whispers a few words to the orderly. When he returns a feeble hand gropes its way towards him, and Hollins looks up appealingly.

"I'm so much weaker. I'm going fast. Would you shake hands, Abbot? What! Then you bear me no ill-will?"

"I do not, Hollins."

The clouding eyes seem to seek his wistfully, wonderingly.

"And yet—I wronged you so."

"Do not think of me. That—all came right."

"I know—I know. It is *her* heart I may have broken—Bessie's. My God! What could she have thought when he came back to her—after seeing you?"

"He told her her lover was dead. I made inquiries."

"Thank God for that! But all the same—she is sorrowing—suffering—and it's all my doing. I believe I could die content, almost happy, if I knew she had not—if I knew—I had not—brought her misery."

13

" Are you sure, Hollins ?"

" Sure! Heaven, yes! Why, Abbot? Do you—do *you* know ?"

" She seems happy, Hollins. She is to be married in the spring; I don't know just when."

There is another moment of intense silence in the little room. Outside the muffled tramp of the night patrols and the gruff challenge of sentries fall faintly on the ear. Within there is only the quick breathing of the sinking man. There is a long, long look from the dying eyes; a slow movement towards the well-nigh pulseless heart. Then comes the sound of heavy feet upon the stair, and presently the uncouth form of Rix is at the threshold, a piteous look in his haggard face. Abbot raises a hand in warning, and glances quickly from the prisoner at the door to the frame whence fast is ebbing the imprisoned soul. The hand that had faintly clasped his is slowly creeping up to the broad and brawny chest, so feeble now. Far across the rippling waters of the Rappahannock the notes of a bugle, prolonged and distant, soft and solemn, float upon the still night air. 'Tis the soldiers' signal " Lights Out !"—the soldiers' rude

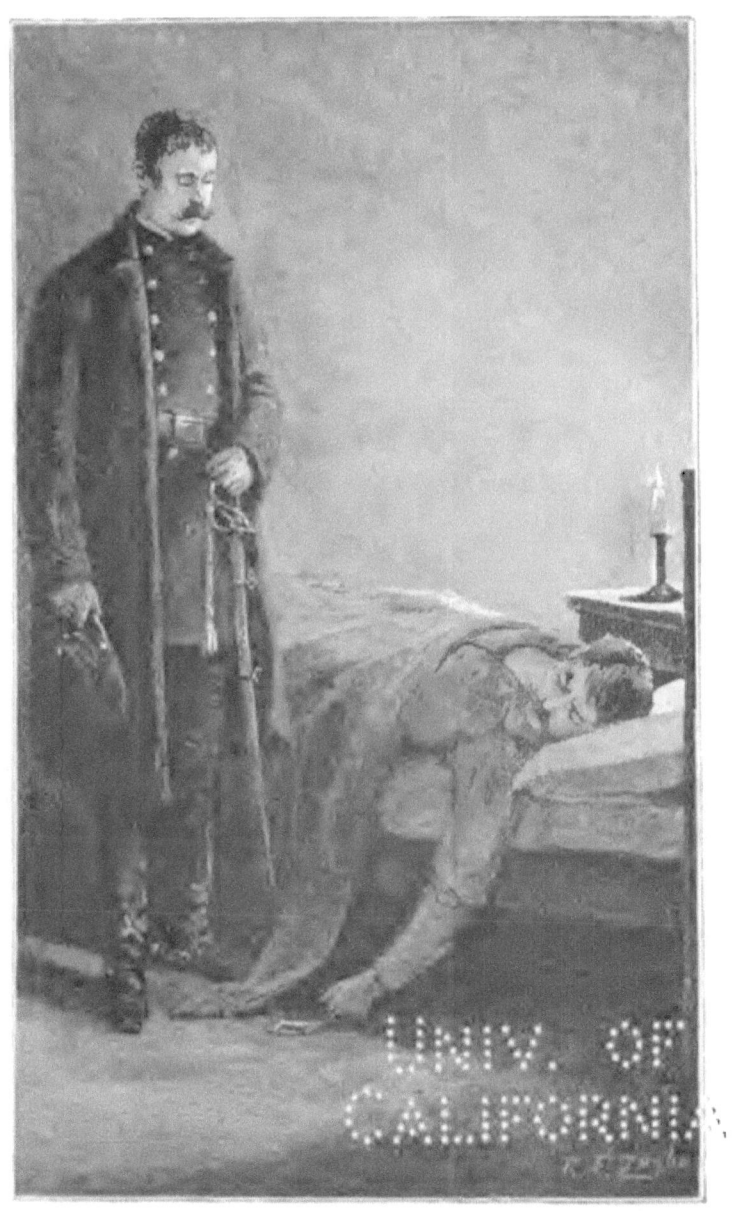

" *Draws forth her precious picture and lays it at a rival's feet.*"

yet never-forgotten lullaby. An instant gleam as of recognition hovers in the glazing eyes. Then follow a few faint gasps; then—one last gesture as the arm falls limp and nerveless; but it draws forth her precious picture and lays it at a rival's feet.

THE END.

www.ingramcontent.com/pod-product-compliance
Lightning Source LLC
Chambersburg PA
CBHW022002050726
47498CB00007BA/2657